Be Blessed & Enjoy! 4/23

Faith Alone

By Terri Ann Johnson

Terri a Johnson

bgb
BROWN GIRLS BOOKS

Houston, Texas * Washington, D.C.

Faith Alone © 2018 by Terri Ann Johnson

Brown Girls Books LLC

www.BrownGirlsBooks.com

ISBN: 978-1-944359-74-4 (ebook)

ISBN: 978-1-944359-75-1 (print)

First Brown Girls Publishing LLC trade printing

Manufactured and Printed in the United States of America

ACKNOWLEDGEMENTS

This has been a dream come true. First and foremost, I want to thank God for guiding me every step of the way. He gave me this vision and the resources that I needed to make it plain.

Thank you to my parents, Lavern and Thelma Johnson, for giving me life and love. You provided me with everything that I needed while growing up and it's never stopped. When I thought about my pen name I landed on several variations. But, I decided on my full name because my Dad calls me Terri Ann. Therefore, my pen name was a no brainer. Mom, thank you for proofing the many rounds of edits.

Joshua, you are my muse. Everything I do, I do for you. Your encouragement means so much. When I'm typing and you run into the room to peep at the laptop and say, "Mommy you're doing good," those special moments pushed me to keep typing no matter how tired I was. Thank-you for your unconditional love, Honey Bunny.

To my sister in heaven, Michele, my love of reading came directly from you. I miss you every day. My main character's name has part of yours, but she has all of your sweet spirit.

To my nieces and nephews, Krystal, Phillip, Christopher, Jr., and Naomi, thank you for the gifts of laughter and fun. I love you and the times that we spend together. Whatever you do in life, do it to the fullest.

To my brother-in-law, Christopher B. Wade, Sr., thank you for sharing your legal insight with me.

To my entire family and all of my friends, thank you for your continued support and belief in me. Your texts, emails, Facebook messages and phone calls, supporting my dream, helped me cross the finish line. Steven Fitchett, you continually asked "Godma when is your book coming out?" Please know that your question motivated me to finish.

To my East Friendship Baptist Church and O.L.Q.P. families, my Seton Sisters, my GWU crew, and my co-workers, past and present, thank you for your support. It means everything to me.

To my sorors in The Federal City Alumnae Chapter, your excitement has meant so much to me. I love you and hope to make you proud throughout my literary journey.

To the sorors in my chapter of initiation, Mu Beta, your youthful exuberance gives me life. To the sorors of the Washington DC Alumnae and the Prince George's County Alumnae Chapters thank-you for your continued support throughout my Delta journey. And to all my sorors of Delta Sigma Theta Sorority, Inc., thank you for your love and support.

To my Sister Scribes in VCM's January 2017 Bootcamp, this novel started in this group and your guidance, support and transparency helped me to complete it. I can't wait to read the work that will come from this collaborative group of women.

To Michelle Cole, Keleigh Hadley and Nicole Lester, thank you for sharing personal information with me so that I could make Lachelle's high risk pregnancy more authentic.

To Patricia Bridewell, Naleighna Kai, Yolanda Gore, and V. Helena, thank-you for helping me to gain exposure as an author and getting my debut novel out to the public.

To J.L. Woodson graphic designer and owner of Woodson Creative Studio, you were easy to work with and the cover took my breath away. I'm looking forward to working with you in the future.

To my Brown Girls Books family, for everything that you do to help BGB authors to get their work out there to the public. Jason Frost, Social Media manager and Norma Warren, Publicist, you guys are, simply, the best. Thank you to each and every staff member at BGB.

To Terry McMillan, you have been my inspiration since *Mama* and my best friend in my head since *Waiting to Exhale*. On top of that we share the same name. Thank you for always being you.

To Rhonda McKnight, my literary Godmom, I love your books. Your class taught me so much and your encouragement makes me smile.

To my squad, LaTonja Belsches, Cheryl Boderick, Chris Hart-Wright, Gwen Jones, Lavern Miles, Tessa Murphy, Nichelle Poe, Diane Smith, Elaine Taylor and Kim Williams, you are the bomb dot com. The career of an author is solitary. Thank-you for being my biggest cheerleaders, making sure that my son is good while I'm working, and ensuring that I stay 'in the mix'.

I want to give an extra big shout-out to my sister and soror, Latreece Johnson Wade and my BFF and soror, Rhonda Pope Brown. Thank-you for giving up your time to troubleshoot ideas with me and for reading and reading and reading *Faith Alone* some more. LOL.

And last, but not least, THANK YOU to the Founders of Brown Girls Books, ReShonda Tate Billingsley and Soror Victoria Christopher Murray, two BAWSE women. Thank you for including me in the *All I Want for Christmas* anthology. You have made dreams come true!

I hope you enjoy *Faith Alone* and please, leave a review. Look out for my next novel. It. Is. Coming.

Faith Alone

Chapter 1

I gripped the pregnancy box in my hand, thinking that telling my husband I might be pregnant should be one of the most exciting days of my life. Keyword: should. I had buried any and all thoughts of motherhood forever.

The sound of my heart beating hammered in my ears. Lying on the couch didn't comfort me. So still holding onto the box, I got up and walked into the kitchen and headed straight to the fridge; but I couldn't eat.

I tried to think: what would I normally be doing while I waited for Brian to come home? Then, I shook that thought away. It didn't matter at this point because there wouldn't be anything normal about the conversation Brian and I would have once he walked through the door.

Part of me thought that maybe I would take care of this by myself, without ever telling him, without him ever finding out. But I learned in my younger years that lies could equal loss. The last thing I wanted to lose was Brian. So it was best for me to honor my vows, best for me to handle this, for better or for worse.

And this part was the worst.

I glanced down at the box and set it in the middle of the dining room table.

He'll see it there, that's for sure.

Then, I staggered back into the living room. But not a second later, a car door slammed, and I jumped up off the couch, stubbing my baby toe on the edge of the coffee table. *Dayum. Dayum. Dayum.*

The pain didn't stop me, though. I raced down the hallway into the dining room, slipping on our polished hardwood floors, but thank God, I didn't fall.

I grabbed the pregnancy test from the table, then dashed up the stairs. Breathing hard, I hid it in our bathroom, tossing it onto the vanity. Then, I took a couple of moments to get settled.

Once my breathing was back to normal, I moseyed down the stairs, a stark contrast to the crazy woman who'd been running around the house a few minutes ago.

Telling him is the best way.

That was what I'd decided. Brian wouldn't play games with me by leaving information sitting on the table, so I didn't want to do that to him. I would tell Brian what I knew: that I was two weeks late for my period and because I'd been so focused on meeting the deadline for the grant I'd just submitted, I hadn't noticed my missed period until this morning.

I had it all worked out in my mind; I knew exactly how we would handle this. But, Brian was a problem-solver. Would my husband try to fix this? Or would he go along with my plan?

By the time I reached the bottom of the stairs, I was surprised that Brian still had not come through the door. I curled up on the leather sectional, pulling my favorite, fuzzy throw blanket over my legs, wanting my husband to find me in my most relaxed state.

Still, no Brian. What was taking him so long? I pushed myself off the couch and peeked out the window. Brian's car wasn't even in the driveway. It must have been a neighbor that I'd heard.

Get it together, Lachelle.

Returning to the sofa, I grabbed the latest edition of O Magazine and tried to focus on Suzie Orman's article, but my thoughts soon wandered. Maybe if I practiced, my words would come out with more confidence. Maybe if I practiced, I wouldn't scare my husband to death.

Taking a breath, I said, "Brian, I have something to tell you." I imagined how I would sit him down, grab his hands and say, "Brian, I'm pregnant."

I practiced those two sentences over and over until it felt ridiculous and then, I turned on the TV. The news droned on and on until the anchor said, "Now, turning to local news, another young girl has been reported missing, here in D.C."

A picture of a girl, no more than thirteen or fourteen, flashed on the screen and I turned the TV off before the anchor could say the girl's name. That was certainly not something I wanted to hear right now.

Before I could find another distraction, I heard the slam of another car door. I froze, though I still wasn't sure if it was Brian until, "Are you working on your rebound, Matt?" my husband asked our teenage neighbor. There was a pause, and then, his voice again. "Yeah, okay, meet me at the gym around noon tomorrow."

I began counting the seconds from him locking the car to walking up the six steps to checking the mailbox. His keys jingled as he opened the door and I was still frozen in place on the sofa.

One, two, three. "Chellllllllle, I'm home."

Once he turned the corner and saw me lying on the couch, he belted out, "I'm just a bachelor, looking for a partner." Brian wiggled his non-rhythmic hips and began moving toward me as though his alter ego's name was B-Fine, because he was fine, all five feet and nine inches of him. He'd played college football, and the girls used to flirt with him, telling him that he looked like Emmitt Smith. It was true; it was his smile and his complexion.

But although he could run that ball, he could never really dance. Usually, if a guy couldn't dance, I would never let him get past first base. Why waste my time? But, Brian was so fine and sweet, and once we became more than friends, he squashed my myth. He proved that just because you didn't have rhythm on your feet, didn't mean you didn't know what do between the sheets.

I forced a smile as he fumbled with the buttons on his shirt.

"Alexa." He called out to our Echo. "Play Ginuwine's Pony." The whole time, his eyes remained on me. Brian pulled and tugged at his cufflinks. You'd think they were glued onto his shirt because they wouldn't come off. But, he didn't care. His goofiness and pretend ineptness was all part of the fun. Then, he crouched down, got on his hands and knees and crawled the rest of the way to the couch.

But right before he reached me, he shouted. "Ouch." He picked through the carpet, then held up the push pin that had stabbed his hand.

I couldn't help but laugh. "Luckily, you only strip for me, babe. Come here and let mama kiss da boo boo."

"Alexa, turn it off. My entertainment for this evening is done." Brian took his shoes off and laid down with me.

We loved this couch. It held the two of us comfortably. I snuggled under his chin. This was my sweet spot.

After a few moments, he said, "Usually my striptease act cracks you up. You okay?"

I should've known that he'd notice a difference in my demeanor.

"I'm okay," I lied.

"Are you hungry? Were you waiting for me to eat? It's so nice outside; I should throw a few things on the grill."

Dinner. "Uhmmm, I hadn't really thought about food." I wished the world would stop right here, right now.

"Well, I know a nice chargrilled steak will put you in the right mood. Let me get up and thaw out two rib-eyes. Can you take out the ingredients for my sauce while I run upstairs?"

As he rolled away from me and sat up, I shouted out, "Brian, I'm pregnant." I had tried.

Keyword: tried.

But I couldn't hold it in any longer. "I'm about two weeks late." Then, I spilled out the rest of the story in one long breath. "I was working so hard on that grant submission for Loving Our Babies that I didn't even think about it until this morning. I stopped at the drug store on my way home and picked up a pregnancy test so that we could take it this evening. I knew you would want to be with me."

His eyes were wide and then, he motioned with his hands. "Chelle, slow down." He shook his head when he said, "So, you don't know that you're pregnant, right? As much birth control as we use, could it really happen?"

I gave him a side-eye. "As much sex as we have, I guess so."

He exhaled a long breath as if he could blow this challenge away. "Well, let's not assume anything. The stress of your job may've contributed to you being late."

As I looked up, directly into his face, I said, "You know I'm never late. I've been stressing about telling you all day."

His silence told me that he was thinking, thinking of a way to fix this.

I sat up and twisted because I wanted to look into his eyes when I whispered, "There's nothing you can do to fix this. It was a mistake. Let's just correct it."

He took another deep breath, then another long exhale before he pushed himself off the couch and picked up his shirt.

They way he leaned against the wall and rubbed his eyes, I knew he was thinking, thinking, thinking.

Then after what felt like too many seconds, he said in the most respectful tone, "It wasn't a mistake. This was God's plan." He slipped back into his shirt, then walked over and knelt in front of me. "What happened to you happened almost twenty-five years ago. Doctors know more now and medical technology has advanced."

I shook my head. "But, I could die," I said through my tears. "I am forty-two years old," I added like I needed to remind him of all the facts. "I have a history of high blood pressure and I had a baby that..."

He didn't let me finish. "Look at me." His voice was so gentle, so full of love. His touch was the same as he wiped my tears, then tilted my chin upward. "No one is dying, no one. Let's take this step by step. We'll take the test tonight and we'll call Doctor Price in the morning. Is that a plan?"

He spoke so assuredly that all I could say was, "Yes."

"My Chelle, you married a man, a man who will stand with you through the storms of life. We have each other and God is on our side."

Brian wiped more of my tears away and moved my natural curls out of my face. When he kissed me, I really thought that everything in my world would now be all right.

Keyword: thought.

Chapter 2

Walking up the steps to the master bathroom felt like I was walking to the gas chamber. Discovering that I might be carrying a life shouldn't feel like death. But, death had been an anchor weighing me down since I became an adult.

This walk was nothing like the one I took to the Planned Parenthood office near my high school during the fall of 1993. When I thought I was pregnant then, I was shocked, but a little excited. I was young and ready to take on the world.

John met me at my locker at lunchtime asking, "Are we doing that thang today, shorty?"

"Yes, the plan has not changed; the sooner the better."

We walked to the cafeteria in silence. His guilt stifled the corny jokes he typically cracked. My stupidity silenced me. It had been the first time for the both of us, and he begged me to let him put it in for only a minute. Little did I know that it would be over in less than a minute. Yet, that minute had been enough. Everything that came out of him, was inside of me.

Once we got to the lunch room, I whispered the plan to him.

I said, "We can go to the Planned Parenthood office in Southwest."

"Shorty, there is one right around the corner from here."

"I don't want everybody knowing my business," I protested. "It won't take us more than fifteen minutes on the bus."

Before taking the last bite of his steak and cheese sandwich, he caved. "Okay, where should I meet you?"

"Meet me at the bus stop right across the street from the main entrance, right after the last bell rings." I thought about how mature he was handling this and added, "John, thank you for going with me."

"Shorty, I got chu. I'm surprised that you didn't ask 'Tough' Tracy to go with you. I feel honored."

I didn't tell him that I hadn't even told my best friend. "This is between you and me, for now."

After school, we got on that bus, headed to Southwest and light music greeted us as we walked into the Planned Parenthood office. I completed the paperwork that the receptionist gave me while John stood at the window pretending to shoot hoops as if we weren't about to find out the most important news of our lives. I couldn't be mad; he was here.

The receptionist ushered me back into what I thought was the doctor's office. Instead, I sat in an examination room for about thirty minutes before a nurse came in. She asked a few questions, took a sample of my blood, and told me to come back in two days.

I obeyed, and forty-eight hours later, John and I found out that we'd become parents in the early summer of 1994.

I was so deep in that memory that I didn't hear Brian come up the steps. As I curled up on our bed, Brian stroked my face, and as if reading my mind, he said, "This isn't like last time."

Brian's love wrapped itself around me like a warm blanket. Although he held me from behind, the smell of his cologne met my nose.

As he wiped a trickle of tears from my cheek, he softly sang, *"I just want to praise you, forever and ever and ever for all you've done for me. Blessings and glory and honor they all belong to you. Thank you, Jesus, for blessing me."* When he got to the last verse of my favorite song, he said, "You wanna join me?"

"Naw, no singing today." It had been a long time since I had been in this kind of funk. Bringing his spirit down was something that I didn't want to do. But, I couldn't fake the fact that I was drowning in a sea of depression. I needed to know if I was pregnant, now.

"Chelle, let's do this," Brian said as though he was talking to the boys on his football team before a game. He grabbed a bottle of water from the nightstand. "Drink some water."

"I don't need it," I said as I pushed off the bed, telling myself to *calm down and be nice.* Brian was doing his best to help me through this, but he had not been a part of my life in high school; he had no idea what it was like to go through the heartache and pain.

But, he is here now.

I grabbed the test from the cabinet and decided to go back into the bedroom to read the instructions with Brian.

Brian's eyes lit up when he saw me stand in the doorway. It was a haphazard toss of the box into the air, but I wasn't surprised at all when he caught it.

"Together?"

"Together." I reassured him.

He gently opened the box and read the instructions to himself. Then he gave me the Cliff Notes version.

It was simple. All I had to do was pee on the stick…and I did.

Chapter 3

Those two little lines from the pregnancy test led us to Dr. Price's office where we waited for her to come in and talk about our situation. She was able to see us on Tuesday, and this was only my second time leaving the house since we'd found out on Friday night.

After the shock of seeing the positive result, I had stayed in just about all weekend. There was no way that I could go out and face the world, go out and be excited. I didn't want to go down the road of loving with all my heart again and having that love drowned in an ocean of tears.

Even though I'd been filled with despair, Brian had done his best to help me. He'd given me space while he picked up what I would normally do: he cooked, cleaned, and made sure that my only responsibility was to relax.

But the most important thing that he did for me — he prayed. As a man of God, he went into his prayer closet, most of Saturday. Then, on Sunday morning, he went into my closet and came out with an outfit for me to wear to church.

Although I didn't want to leave the house, I knew it was the right thing.

Brian told me, "We'll get up and watch God do the rest."

The Word said that 'faith and fear cannot dwell in the same place'. Brian did his best to remind me of that.

The tap on Dr. Price's door brought me back to this mild and sunny and frightening Tuesday morning.

"Good morning." Dr. Price walked in holding medical folders. As she put them down on her desk, she greeted us with a warm smile.

"Mr. and Mrs. Jackson," Dr. Price began with her hands folded on top of her desk. She wore a smile as she told me the worst news. "Mrs. Jackson, you are pregnant."

Brian bowed his head and said, "Thank you, Lord."

The doctor glanced at Brian with a smile, but when she faced me, I saw her concern. My silence made her stand, walk around to the other side of her desk, and sit down in a chair next to me.

"I know your medical history, and I hope that you will remain positive," Dr. Price said as she stroked my back.

I gave her a slight smile, the same smile that I'd given Brian all weekend.

That was the only response this news could elicit from me. Because I'd been here before and my happiness had been snatched away, stolen from me when I'd lost my baby.

"Doctor Price, could Lachelle or the baby be in any danger?" He didn't give the doctor a chance to respond before he continued, "Because, I've researched preeclampsia. I read that there are various factors that contribute to the condition and it might not strike a woman twice." Brian reached for my hand. The look in his charcoal gray eyes was serious. The smile that usually lit up his face, always displaying his pearly whites was not present.

"Well, one thing that many people don't know about preeclampsia is that it is most often seen in first-time pregnancies, in teens, and in women over forty," the doctor said. "When you were eighteen-years-old, you fit two of those three categories. So, that would explain what happened to you before. But I have to be honest. Since you've experienced a stillbirth in the past, your pregnancy is high risk by default."

"What does that mean?" Brian asked.

"Your wife is at a higher risk, but because of what we know, we will monitor Lachelle more often." Dr. Price looked at me and continued. "You'll visit us more often, and we'll run more tests. And we'll assign you to specialists who will look after you as well. We'll discuss the signs of preeclampsia before you leave today."

"Have any of your patients had a medical history similar to mine?"

There was so much compassion in her eyes and in her voice when she said, "Yes, and she is alive and well and so is her three-year-old son." She paused, giving us time to think about that.

A son. That woman had a son.

Dr. Price said, "I have a preliminary plan in mind for you. Usually, around thirty-seven weeks we may induce labor or perform a cesarean section. This usually keeps preeclampsia from getting worse, if we see the onset of it."

"I've been praying all weekend that this appointment would bring us hope," Brian said, and by this time, the gleam in his eyes had returned, and his smile brightened the room.

I placed my hand on my belly. Brian placed his hand over mine.

Dr. Price said, "There is hope. We determine when to deliver the baby on how far along you are in your pregnancy, how well the fetus is doing and the severity of the preeclampsia. We'll do everything we can to get you to week thirty-seven and make our decision as a team. But remember, this is if you even develop preeclampsia."

Keyword: If.

After listening to Dr. Price, I didn't know how I felt. I'd walked in here so scared that I would lose another baby. Even now, I remembered how much I'd loved my little honey bear like I'd loved nothing else. He'd been my hope; he'd been my joy. I had wrapped up so much love in our future together, a future that never came to fruition. I knew that I didn't want to experience that kind of loss again.

After losing my baby and dealing with depression, I promised myself that I would help women get through the journey of pregnancy. I'd created programs that helped reduce the low birth rate, infant illness, and even death. The most fulfilling part of my job had been the friendships developed with the moms and babies who I watched grow through the years. Most of the women that we served were young; about the same age I was when I got pregnant. Most were scared, just like I was. But, I was an example that a setback didn't prevent you from bouncing back. I'd served as a program manager for the non-profit organization, Loving Our Babies. Sometimes, I'd assist with writing grants. I loved my role as surrogate sister or auntie. But now, it was all about to change.

"Chelle, you've been quiet. What are you thinking?" Brian said as he stroked my cheek.

"This is a lot to take in. You know I wasn't feeling this at all. You look happy." I shoved Brian's shoulder to let him know that he could be okay with this.

Brian's only response: he picked up my hand and gently kissed my wedding ring. The glimmer in his eyes told me that I was correct. Brian was a father figure to many boys he coached, current and previous players. He nurtured, mentored and yes...loved. He'd made a difference; many of the boys and young men didn't have a sense of family and Brian provided that. We hosted many a cook-out where Brian taught the boys life skills, taught them how to work to impress God, their parents and their teachers.

He made sure that the boys understood that men were measured by the way they treated the women in their lives. Brian walked that walk. He treated me the way God intended for a man to treat a woman. He set the example.

"I'll leave you two now." Dr. Price stood. "I'll have my nurse come in and give you some literature and make your next appointment." The way she paused, I knew she wanted us to really hear her next words. "Mr. and Mrs. Jackson, please know that my team and I stand ready to do everything we can to ensure a positive outcome, a healthy baby."

We stood, and I hugged Dr. Price, feeling the optimism in her heart. Brian tried to shake her hand, but Dr. Price said, "I'm old school, give me a hug."

We all laughed.

"Thank you, Doctor Price," Brian began after he stepped back. "Thank you for your encouragement. I know we'll see each other often this year and I'm ready to do whatever I need to do to make sure that Lachelle and the baby remain healthy."

"I know you will take great care of them." She left us with one last message. "With God all things are possible. I'll see you soon."

When we were alone, Brian turned to me. "Babe, I hope you're feeling a little lighter because I am."

I nodded.

"I'm starved. I didn't eat anything this morning. Why don't we stop and get some lunch before we head home? I told the school that I wouldn't be coming in today. We can spend some time talking about what Doctor Price told us. You did tell the office that you would be out all day, didn't you?" Brian looked at me as though he was my father, chastising me for being a workaholic.

"Yes. I. Did." I responded, punctuating each syllable. "I feel a little relief. But, we can talk over lunch."

A look of contemplation rested on Brian's face, in his furrowed eyebrows and tightened lips. "I want to thank God right here in this office before we leave." He turned my torso to face his and took my hands. He closed his eyes and went to the throne of grace.

"Father God, we thank you for what you have done and everything that you are about to do. We thank you for your grace and your mercy. Together we recite what we know to be true."

I knew which scripture we would pray. Jeremiah twenty-nine and eleven was our favorite. In unison, we prayed right up in Dr. Price's office.

"For I know the plans I have for you, declares the Lord, plans to prosper you and not harm you, plans to give you hope and a future."

Brian completed our prayer. "We ask these and all blessings in the name of your Son Jesus Christ. Amen."

A cheerful, "Amen," flowed from my lips.

"I love you, Mrs. Jackson."

"Yeah, I know." I said.

As Brian slid my jacket over my shoulders, I eased my arms around his waist, lifted my head and gave him a slow, long kiss.

"Uhmmmm, does that mean you love me back?"

"Always and forever."

Chapter 4

Heading east on Pennsylvania Ave, I asked Brian to ride past the White House. "You never know, we might see Barack or Michelle," I said, adjusting my seat so that I could lie back a little. Although the sun wasn't burning as hot as it would be in a few weeks, it was bright, so I pulled my sunglasses from the glove compartment.

The tourists were out in full effect. School had just let out for the summer in many parts of the country, as evidenced by the many families riding Segways. There were long lines at the food and ice cream trucks.

As we passed the new African-American Museum, Brian asked, "What do you want to eat?"

Turning up Jill Scott on the radio gave me something to do while I thought about it. "I'll let you choose. You've accommodated me all weekend."

Brian smiled that smile. "Well then…you know I want some hood food."

"Am I supposed to be eating hood food?" He knew that I loved a good steak and cheese sandwich or chicken wings with mambo sauce. I was happy that my appetite had returned and my taste buds were talking.

"I think you'll be okay. We can call it our last supper of hood food." His laugh was infectious.

"Okay, let's go to the new Ben's Chili Bowl on H Street. That's upscale hood food."

I side eyed him. "A hot dog ain't never upscale. I don't care where it's coming from. But, I'm good with Ben's."

We headed toward H Street, in the Northeast section of the city, where Brian was raised. It was within a few blocks of Ben's that one of the most horrific rape/murder cases had taken place in 1984, reminiscent of the Central Park Five Case in New York City.

Now, there were new office buildings, restaurants, and bars sitting next to run down storefronts; signs of gentrification were everywhere. Gone were the streets strewn with litter and in were the streetcars. Cranes reaching up to the sky filled empty holes that were once affordable homes. Boys with sagging pants ran past a middle-aged, white woman walking her dog. When we saw white folks walking down H Street, we knew the city was changing.

"Black folks riding bikes now?" I asked sarcastically after I saw the orange bike racks that city dwellers could rent.

Brian shook his head. "You know those bikes aren't for us. They wouldn't trust us to put 'em back."

"It's all a part of changing the 'hood. Or should I say changing who lives in the 'hood?"

As we made the left onto H Street, the block was filled with a throng of people hanging out, not harming anyone, but not doing anything constructive either.

The brightness of the sun couldn't compare to the yellow and red interior of the newest Ben's Chili Bowl, a stark contrast to the original diner (the epitome of a greasy spoon) that had been around since 1958. T-shirts and hats with Ben's logo were for sale, lined up in a glass case. There were a few millennials eating while working on tablets. The owner, Mrs. Ali, was there giving a little boy a balloon as he left with his family.

The history of the diner sat emblazoned at the top of the wall above a window looking out onto H Street; it's opening in 1958, the 1963 March on Washington, the 1968 riots, through the years to opening four additional diners around the city. Although this was a new location, nostalgia greeted us as we walked through the door. Pictures in black wooden frames adorned the walls – Presidents Obama and Clinton, D.C. politicians, Hollywood stars, members of D.C. Go-Go bands, and of course, D.C.'s Mayor for Life, Marion Barry - were lined up closer to the back of the diner. I was happy that the new location brought the nostalgia of the old one. The unmistakable smell of grilled hotdogs filled the air.

A big guy, with an even bigger smile, resembling an NFL linebacker, stepped up and greeted Brian. "What's up, B? I haven't seen you in a while."

"Man, everything is good with me. I see things are even better with you, wearing the manager's outfit. No more white apron for you, huh?"

"Oh, I whip it out when I need to. It gets busy on the weekends."

Dre. The old grill master. Yes, he worked at the original Ben's on U Street calling customers by name and their orders as they walked through the door. A few of my work colleagues loved Ben's Chili Bowl, and I remembered Dre from when I went with them.

"Yeah, loyalty pays off. The Ali's are like family. Getting my job right out of high school kept me off the streets. But what about you? I hear you putting in work with your football teams. And I hear you might be running for Advisory Neighborhood Commissioner. They couldn't find a better brotha to get some things done."

Local civic leaders regarded Brian as the best person to represent our little section of the city. Everyone loved his commitment to the kids, the city's future.

"Yeah, I decided to do it. I couldn't keep talkn' about it and not be about it."

"Yo B, don't hesitate to come back and bring posters or flyers, whateva you need to get it done.

Dre looked around to see where he'd seat us. "Do you prefer a table or booth?"

"I'm not sure where my manners went," Brian said as he put his arm around me. "This is my wife, Lachelle. Lachelle this is Dre. We know each other from…" They looked at each other, laughed and responded in unison. "From back in the day."

"Okay, well I know to leave that alone. It's nice meeting you, Dre. This new Ben's is nice."

The shiny, red cushions covering the chairs and booths could've been delivered yesterday they were so new. In the back of the diner was a full-size jukebox looking like it was delivered straight from the *Happy Days* set. It added to the authenticity of it being more of a diner than a restaurant.

"We'll take that booth in the back." Brian said nodding his head toward it.

"You go up and order; it's on the house. I'll put water in your booth so no one will sit there. You see how crowded we are." Dre gave us a sarcastic smile.

We expected a lunchtime crowd, but we were two of about ten people that day.

Before Dre went to get our drinks, he and Brian gave each other that grip that most brothers use to say hello or goodbye.

Before they broke their grip, I heard Brian ask the question that I had thought about. "Bill Cosby didn't make it onto the wall of fame?"

"Naw B, Cosby didn't make it up. Mrs. Ali didn't want any problems.

After we ordered our food, we walked to our booth. The sparkles in the yellow tile caught my eye. Two afternoon sports prognosticators debated the latest rounds of the NBA playoffs on a plasma screen that had to be at least sixty inches wide.

We couldn't wait to bite into those chili dogs. As I wiped sauce from the side of Brian's mouth, he looked into my eyes. "How are you feeling?"

Dr. Price's optimism must've been contagious. "Actually, not as stressed as before."

Creases formed on his forehead as he looked down at his food. I knew he was trying to ascertain the best way to proceed.

"What's on your mind?" I asked.

"You know…" He took a deep breath. "We've been married for twelve years, knowing each other since we were in our mid-twenties. I've always respected your stance on not having children. I knew that God ordained our marriage and I wouldn't trade it for anything in the world."

I heard a *but* coming. He inhaled and exhaled.

"But, we've never talked about Christian."

My heart raced, and I took a sip of water to calm it down. Brian knew my baby's name melted my heart. After I told him about that time in my life, I reiterated that I didn't want to regurgitate the story. He never mentioned it again or his name. Until today. No one ever said his name. My baby's name.

Before I could finish chewing what was left of the hotdog and ask him, 'why are you doing this today?' Brian slid his arm across the table and stroked my hand; a sign of peace.

"Don't get upset. I just think that before we begin this journey, we have to talk through the hurt and pain that Christian's loss caused you."

I knew what he meant, but I was stubborn. Leaning back in the booth, I blurted my truest feelings. "What's there to talk about?"

I could see the compassion in his eyes. "I don't know how to say this, but I believe that you may feel that having another baby would be like cheating on Christian."

He stopped speaking as if to let his words settle in. It was painful to admit, and I wasn't sure if I would use those words, but Brian was hitting on something. My baby was stillborn. I had so many plans; plans for our future. Was it something that I did? Was there something that I didn't do that caused the stillbirth? I was eighteen years old.

Brian wanted to know, so I took him back to the summer of 1993.

The guilt of getting pregnant almost stopped me from saying anything to my mother.

Keyword: almost

I knew that she loved me like she'd given birth to me. But I was still afraid to tell her. I wasn't the only girl at school pregnant, but I was the one that people looked upon with pity because it wasn't supposed to happen to me. They'd tell me; 'bad things happen to good people.' Once I told my mother I believed that she shared those sentiments.

My baby hadn't moved in a few days. "Mom I need to go to the doctor, I haven't felt the baby move lately."

She moved but not with the volition that I would've liked to see from my mom. It was like she took me because I needed a ride.

Once we arrived, they rushed me to the back, took all kinds of tests and did a sonogram. The doctor listened and felt. His widened eyes gave me the ominous news. He pushed my tummy. "Move on your other side, dear."

As he assisted me to my right side, I felt hot and light headed. I was sure the doctor thought that I had already fainted because he stopped speaking directly to me, and began using pronouns.

"Her blood pressure has skyrocketed."

"We have to focus on saving her."

Saving her?

Swerving in and out of consciousness or maybe dreaming, I heard what sounded like a rush of people. Through slits in my eyes, I saw nurses and doctors hovering over me shouting, "Anesthesia." Then, "C-section."

After that, I must've fallen back to sleep because in a dream I heard the faint sound of a baby's cry.

A beeping sound woke me out of an unsettled slumber. I wasn't in the same room. This one smelled so sterile. It was stark white except for the brown chair that my mother sat in.

"Lachelle." My mother rose to her feet making her way to my bed. As she grabbed my hand, a single tear rolled down her face.

"Where's my baby? I want to see my baby."

"It was a little boy, but he didn't make it, honey."

My eyes must've asked, 'didn't make it?'

"He was gone before we even got here."

With pain etched on my mother's face, she continued. "Your blood pressure increased so quickly the doctors thought that we might lose you."

After what seemed like a minute, I asked the question that I knew the answer to.

"Can I see my baby boy?"

While stroking my forehead, she shook her head. "He's gone, honey." I turned my head toward the window and thought about the toes that I couldn't count, the hair that I couldn't stroke and the cheeks that I couldn't kiss.

Tears welled up in my eyes. As I picked up a napkin to dab them, Brian gently stroked my other hand. I smiled, letting him know that I was okay.

"I just think that it's time to mourn him. And time to talk to him; tell him how much losing him hurt. Tell him how much you love him and that you'll never forget him." Brian hesitated before continuing, "I think the perfect way to begin is by visiting Christian."

At this point, I didn't know what to say. I placed my elbows on the table, folded my hands and rested my forehead on them. Seconds passed, which seemed like minutes. I raised my head, and with what felt like tears flowing from my mouth, I responded. "You can't be serious. You want me to visit his grave?"

"No, I want us to visit him. It will be the beginning of the healing process."

I had never thought about visiting Christian's grave. Not even after twenty-three years.

"We can do it. And with God, all things are possible." This. Man. Here. He was willing to help me process my way through the stillbirth of a baby that he didn't even father. Did they still make men like him? I looked at Brian, I mean really looked at him, seeing his strength, his optimism, and his fortitude.

Brian picked up our trays. "Let's go home, we'll talk more later."

"Okay, I'll run to the ladies room."

"I'll bring the car around to the front."

Before I entered the bathroom, I watched Brian as he walked toward the door. His five foot, nine frame fit his sweatsuit nicely. The muscles in his arms…OMG. I loved this man.

After washing my hands, I looked into the mirror and smiled. For the first time, I saw hope in my eyes. Brian gave me hope, and I believed that this would happen. *I'm having a baby.*

Before I left the bathroom, I touched up my lips with a little more color. Colorful is how I felt and when I got outside, I wanted Brian to see the difference. He needed to see my optimism for our future. I couldn't do this without him. He'd been my rock, my helpmate. His strength transferred to me and as long as he was my man, I knew I'd be good.

As I pulled the ladies room door open and walked toward the front door, I heard a man scream, "You looking at dat nigga?" The angered scream came from outside.

As I got closer to the front door, I looked outside of the huge rectangle window as did everyone else. As Brian leaned against the passenger car door waiting for me to come out, a young man confronted a woman, and in an instant, I made the assumption that was his girlfriend.

Without giving her a chance to respond, the fury in his eyes must've traveled down his arm and into his hand because he cold cocked her in the face.

After that, the world moved in slow motion.

Brian leaped in an attempt to catch the woman but her legs withered and she dropped straight to the ground. Brian knelt to assist her, but, the man grabbed Brian by the back of his sweat jacket. "Get off her."

Brian broke loose from the man's grip and landed an upper cut. His attacker stepped back and threw a jab, that would've landed on Brian's left cheek, but he blocked the blow.

Dre ran past me toward the door. "Somebody call the police!"

As if I became a statue, my legs wouldn't allow me to move, but my eyes never left Brian.

Before Dre crossed the threshold of the door, we heard a loud *boom*. Everyone in the restaurant scurried for cover.

Before I could scream, "Briiiiannnn," he hit the ground and I heard Marvin Gaye croon, *Mercy, mercy me.*

Chapter 5

It was a May day that rivaled the heat of August, and the main chapel of Divine Restoration Christian Ministries was standing room only. DRCM hadn't seen a crowd like this since Deacon Moss had passed away a few years ago. We knew Brian's funeral would be crowded, but this turnout spoke volumes about the man Brian was.

Keyword: was.

That thought made my mind drift back to his final moments.

As Marvin Gaye continued to croon, I watched the man pull out a gun and then, I was almost sure that I saw the bullet as it careened toward Brian's chest. Brian's back hit the ground and that was when I was able to move my legs. I ran out the door, knelt down beside him on the sidewalk and cupped the back of his head in my hands.

Brian made a futile effort to say my name.

Although I heard the sirens blazing in the background, I still screamed. "Somebody get help!" I kissed him and kissed him, and I kissed him some more. My tears covered his face.

I heard the screech of tires; the ambulance coming to a halt. I also felt Brian slipping away. His eyes opened for a final time, and we locked gazes. Then he seemed to fall asleep. The paramedics moved me out of the way, but my spirit knew Brian was gone. I let them do what they needed to do, but I rubbed the top of his head.

As the paramedics moved Brian to the ambulance, Dre whispered to me. "I'm going with you to the hospital. Do you want to ride with me?"

After shaking my head I was able to utter. "I'm riding with Brian."

"Then I'll meet you there." He responded.

After what seemed like not quite an hour, a young African-American man, dressed in blood-stained scrubs came into the waiting room.

Dre and I jumped to our feet.

"Are you Mrs. Jackson?"

Before I answered his question, I asked him a question. "Is my husband...?"

"Mrs. Jackson, I'm so sorry. But, your husband didn't make it out of surgery."

Brian was pronounced dead at the Washington Hospital Center on Monday, May 30, 2016, at 2:25 pm.

If there was a line drawn in the sand of my life, I'd say that there was my life with Brian and now my life after Brian.

The sound of the paper church fans waving back and forth brought my mind back into the sanctuary that only seated three hundred and fifty people. It was filled to capacity. The overflow room in the basement was opened to accommodate our guests. I'd never seen so many children at a funeral, and most of them were crying. I recognized most of Brian's players. But they all seemed to become one wearing their green camouflaged t-shirts emblazoned with Brian's handsome face with angel wings set on a background of blue sky and white clouds.

I was holding up okay until at least twenty boys came up to the pulpit. The spokesman for the group was Trey Johnson. When he first started playing for Brian, he was a little terrorist to the other boys. Brian kept saying, 'All he needs is some guidance.' Brian stuck close to him as he aged and perfected his skills.

After wiping the sweat from his forehead, Trey pulled a piece of paper from his pants pocket, but after glancing at it, he folded it up and placed it into his shirt pocket whispering to himself, but loud enough for us to hear. "I can do this from my heart." Then his voice projected into the microphone. "Hello everyone. My name is Trey Johnson, and we are here to express how much Coach Brian meant to us. Personally, I could call him any time of the day for advice. I'm not only talking about football advice; I'm talking about life. My father wasn't around as I grew up. But, Coach Brian was that father figure who spoke life into my dreams. I may not get the opportunity to play in the NFL but I am on a four-year academic scholarship, playing football and I'm a leader with the Student Government Association at South Carolina State University."

The church erupted in applause.

Once the applause settled, he finished his tribute, looking directly at Brian's casket he spoke through tears. "Coach B, the time, the guidance and the love won't die with you. I'll continue to give to my little brothas just like you gave to me."

Trey was exactly what Brian knew he could be; a model and mentor for the younger boys.

Trey continued. "A few of the younger soldiers want to speak."

Brian's football team was named the Northeast Soldiers. Trey began to lift a little boy up to the microphone, but a deacon brought a step stool up and sat it behind the podium.

He blew into the microphone before starting to speak. "Hello, my name is Isaiah Glover, and I am one of Coach

Brian's soldiers." That's when his sobbing began. Trey and a few others consoled him. He continued. "Coach B was like a father to me. He made me laugh, and he helped me do better in school. I'll miss you, Coach." He turned and hugged Trey.

Allowing my chin to rest on my chest, I closed my eyes after seeing one of the teenagers grip the hand of one of the younger boys.

Brian's legacy would live on through these boys.

As another young man moved to the microphone to speak about the virtues of my husband, I opened my eyes and stared at my belly. Brian's legacy was speaking at the podium, but I carried his true legacy inside of me. I placed my hand on my belly and wondered: what about our baby? Could I do this on my own? I wasn't sure because every child needed a father. A boy needed a man to emulate, and a girl needed a man to show her how to be treated. Would our baby grow up resenting being raised by me, a single mother?

The mayor was the last person to give remarks. Mayor Bowser prided herself on knowing most of the grassroots community leaders.

"I came today to pay my respects to one of the pillars of this community. But, the young men have said it all. There is no greater testament to the man Brian was, than the testimonies of our future leaders. I can't attend everything in the city, but I had to be here today. Brian was someone who I could call to represent me. I'll miss him."

As the mayor spoke, my feelings ranged from depression, anger and grief. During the days that had passed since his murder, those emotions kept me from focusing on the details of planning Brian's funeral.

But, I thank God for my girls, Tracy and Vanessa.

Tracy, sitting on my right, wiped my tears. Vanessa, sitting on my left, encouraged me with gentle rubs on my back.

Tracy was my oldest friend and Vanessa, my sorority sister, flew in from L.A. Without them, I wasn't sure what would've happened to Brian. They'd gone with me to the funeral home and arranged everything there. Then, they'd picked Brian's suit, the purple and white flowers adorning his casket and designed the layout for the colorful program. They stood by me, wiping away every one of my tears, knowing all of my feelings. Well, not every feeling — they didn't know about the baby; if I was gonna tell anyone it would've been them. But, I had to get through this week before I could tell anyone.

The one person missing was Brian's mother. As the choir stood to sing *Going Up Yonder*, I thought back to the only thing I was able to accomplish last week which was visiting her at the assisted living residence. Since I'd lost my mom in my twenties, Mrs. Jackson, or 'Ma' as I affectionately called her, treated me like a daughter, never calling me her daughter-in-law. I felt that I needed to visit her face-to-face to tell her, although her memory had started deteriorating three years ago due to Alzheimer's.

The sunlight filtering through the window shade reflected on Ma's cheek. The steady pace of her chest moving up and down told me that she was having a peaceful day. After I tripped over the leg of the chair, her eyes shot open and they stayed open without blinking.

Turning her head toward the sound, I walked closer to the bed. "Ma, how are you?"

The compassion on her face told me that Brian had already been here to visit his Mom, telling her before I could.

Reaching up for my hand, she whispered, "Lache..." A single tear escaped her eye.

"I'm okay, Ma. How are you?" I sat there for a minute, processing what I'd say, stroking her hands. "Ma, Brian's with God now."

Her lips turned upward, a slight smile. I stood and stroked her soft, white hair a glowing contrast to her cocoa complexion.

I lulled her back to sleep with one of her favorite tunes, my rendition of I Won't Complain.

After I knew she was sleep, through a sea of tears, I continued to sing.

"I ask a question, Lord, why so much pain?"

Walking around her room ensuring that everything was in place, I continued to sing.

"But He knows what's best for me."

By the time I got to "So I'll just say thank you, Lord, I won't complain," I was curled up rocking myself back and forth in the comfortable, plush chair that Brian had purchased and carried in here a few years ago.

I composed myself and wiped cold water over my face. Tracy was waiting outside to take me home and I didn't want her fussing over me.

Leaving the room, I heard Keisha before I saw her. "Has anyone checked on my mama lately? Y'all just sitting around here doing nothing."

Keisha had a knack for telling everyone what they should do but couldn't seem to find her path.

"And look at you sitting over there looking like a broke down Beyonce. You ain't come to work to be cute, did you?"

"Keisha." I called out in an attempt to stop her rant. These employees treated Mrs. Jackson like she was their mother. Keisha's antics could cause that to change.

"Oh, I should've known that you'd be here before me. Don't you think my mother should've heard about her son from her real daughter?"

Her venom spewed more than normal.

"Keisha…"

She stopped me before I could continue. Stepping closer to me, she revealed her truest feelings. Her words were no surprise. "Me, my mother and Brian, it was always the three of us; until you came into the picture. I wanted to tell her about Brian. My big brother is gone. He was like a father to me. But you took him away when y'all got married. And now you're trying to take my mother. I ain't having it."

"Brian was taken from all of us." My voice didn't spew anger, but she knew I wasn't having it either.

Her eyes darted around the lobby, and her body language toned down.

"I'm leaving now. We're leaving the house at nine o'clock on Friday morning if you would like to ride with us. I hope you do. I know you don't like me, but I don't have anything against you."

She didn't respond. But, I felt the need to tell her what was on my heart. "I love you."

I knew not to make any physical contact, even though I wanted to hug her. As I walked out of the door, I felt her eyes following me.

As Pastor Smith wrapped up the eulogy, I laid my head on Vanessa's shoulder. She stroked my cheek and brought me out of my mental fog with a simple question. "Are you alright?"

I answered her with a shrug.

Trying not to focus on Brian's casket, I looked around the pews and as inconspicuous as they tried to be, I noticed the detectives and the undercover police officers. *Is this my new normal?*

Police officers and detectives asked me question after question. It seemed that I was able to remember more in my dreams than when they questioned me; waking up drenched in sweat, screaming Brian's name, Tracy and Vanessa running into my room holding me, praying with me, helping me to get back to sleep.

Keisha's scream brought me out of my daze. "My brother." She tried to run to Brian's casket as the pallbearers began to carry it out of the church. Someone, whom I assumed was her boyfriend, held her back. I prayed that she didn't fall because we would've seen everything under her short skirt. She finally relented and laid in his arms. The sadness that filled her moaning was heart-wrenching.

I was sad, too, but right now probably more mad, no beyond mad. I wanted that fool caught. He'd taken my life away, my love away from me. I'd never find that unconditional love again. I didn't care what we needed to do, Brian's murderer would be caught and have his day in court.

Chapter 6

"M.J., don't slam cousin Lachelle's screen door like that." Brian's cousin Karen screamed as one of her twin sons ran from the kitchen into the backyard.

"Chelle, just say the word, and I'll throw these ninjas out." Tracy non-whispered to me. She was the epitome of my 'ride or die chick'; I was Louise to her Thelma. We had been friends since Marcus Jones was teasing me in the fourth grade at Our Lady of Eternal Peace Elementary School and she blackened his eye. Even though we'd just met, she said she couldn't stand him and was waiting for a reason to whack him.

I had recently moved to Anacostia with my foster mother and father, who eventually adopted me. Since I didn't have any sisters or brothers, Tracy became family.

Before I could respond, she almost dived to save one of my favorite floor lamps from crashing after the other twin bumped into it. Tracy dashed behind him, grabbing the back of his shirt. All I saw were his little legs *running* in the air. A chuckle escaped my mouth for the first time in days.

Since the day of Brian's murder, all I wanted to do was to curl up in my bed and die, too. But, I didn't want anyone feeling sorry for me.

Vanessa needed to catch the red-eye back to L.A. tonight. My line sister was an up and coming actress, trying her best to become the next Taraji P. Henson. She'd majored in acting when we were at Howard University, minoring in musical theatre. My girl could 'sang.' Although she was the quintessential valley girl, she'd created a t-shirt that read, 'Yes, I'm Black. Yes, it's my hair. And no, don't touch'. Even as her straight, black hair adorned her flawless brown skin, Tracy often called Vanessa a 'blond.'

Vanessa grew up attending the most prestigious private schools, and her parents paid full freight. Her family owned a chain of fried chicken fast food joints in L.A.

Standing at the counter in the kitchen, overlooking my dining room, I noticed Vanessa making small talk with my church family, so many of them huddled in the den watching TV. The way they looked at her, I could tell some seemed to recognize her, but couldn't place from where.

Sister Maxine eventually placed where she had seen Vanessa. "You were one of the victims in the TV show *Criminal Minds*, weren't you?" She didn't even give Vanessa a chance to answer before she asked for Vanessa's autograph.

"I'm not really famous." Vanessa said.

"You're famous to me." Sister Maxine said as she pulled a napkin and pen from her purse and pushed both in Vanessa's face.

Vanessa obliged, and of course, they took a selfie.

As the talk show *Ellen* went off, I heard the early evening news coming on. My knees buckled when I saw Brian's face on the screen, causing me to drop a plate in the sink.

Every eye turned to me, and Brother Dwight shouted. "Turn off the TV!"

"No." I said, though my voice wasn't as loud as his. "Leave it on." Now, all eyes turned away from me, and we focused on the television. The reporter stood on the corner of 11th and H Streets in Northeast.

"I'm Shamari Stone, and I'm standing outside of Ben's Chili Bowl in N.E. where a man was gunned down last week rushing to the aid of a woman in an apparent domestic dispute. His funeral was held today."

The camera spanned the restaurant as children jumped in hoping for their five seconds of fame.

Shamari continued. "Police are asking that anyone who knows this man, Jeffrey Bryant, to come forward as he is a person of interest in this case. Again if you see this man, please contact the Metropolitan Police Department."

Person of interest. Pacing the kitchen from the breakfast nook to the stove, I thought I said, "A *person of interest,*" in my head, but when everyone's eyes turned to me, I knew I hadn't.

That was him. I'd never forget that face.

Sister Maxine pushed her tray table to the side and walked into the kitchen. As she reached to hug me, I was fixated on the TV because to my surprise the Chief of Police exited the restaurant.

Shamari hurried over to get an update. "Chief Thomas, have there been any breaks in the case? What's the current status of the investigation?"

"Shamari, as we reported, Jeffrey Bryant is a person of interest in this case. We'd like to talk to him. If anyone provides information that leads to the conviction of a suspect, there is a ten thousand dollar reward."

"Thank you, Chief Thomas."

The Chief of Police nodded and made his way through the people to his car.

Shamari continued. "We now know that there is a ten thousand dollar reward for any information leading to a conviction in this case. I'm Shamari Stone with NBC-4 news."

The city had a lot at stake to ensure that the gentrified areas were safe. I understood that. *But, who put up the reward money?* I knew the city didn't put up that much money for the death of a black man. No one had said anything to me about requesting donations for a reward; not the coaches, not the school, not the Men's fellowship at church.

"Sister Lachelle." Brother Dwight called out. "Did you know about the reward money?" He was one of the men closest to Brian at church. He was also a veteran of the Metropolitan D.C. Police Department.

I shook my head. "I have no idea who posted it."

Brother Dwight walked over to the kitchen where Sister Maxine and I were standing. I knew that he wanted to speak with me with more privacy. Sister Maxine must've sensed it, too. She filled her plate with chicken wings and rejoined the other church members in the den.

Turning to look back to ensure that no one was listening, he whispered. "You know that I'm doing everything I can to get information on the investigation. I can tell you that the woman Brian protected, told the investigators who he was but that she didn't know where he was hiding."

I'd like to think that if I were in her shoes, I would've told them everything I knew; where he hung out, who his running buddies were, anything to help bring closure to the family of the man who'd saved my life.

Brother Dwight's next comment brought me back to our conversation. "Sister Lachelle, we're determined to bring that fool in, dead or alive."

Dead or alive. No, I wanted to see him alive. The man that took my life away from me, I wanted to see him.

"I hope he's brought in alive. I want him to go to trial and sit in jail for as long as he can for killing Brian. Death would be too easy, too quick."

As Brother Dwight nodded, the reward money stayed on my mind. It seemed that someone had a vested interest in the capture of Brian's murderer. But, who?

Chapter 7

Tracy stayed with me for a few days. At a certain point, I wanted to be alone. If my mama was still here, she'd take care of me like I was a baby. If my daddy were still alive, he'd be out on the streets asking people what they knew about Brian's murder. I knew that Tracy and Vanessa cared for me and I guessed after a few days, I was finally ready to talk. But, first I needed to eat.

As I walked down the steps, I noticed the wilted, funeral flowers, sad and lifeless. How appropriate. Then I walked into the kitchen and opened the refrigerator. I couldn't believe all of the food that was still here, even though the funeral was five days ago. The baby had to eat; I kept reminding myself. The paper plates that piled up on my nightstand betrayed my normal, spotless home. Cleaning would wait.

As I struggled to open the living room window to let some fresh air in, I saw Tracy's car swerve around the corner to park outside of my house. I stood there watching as she slammed the car door and marched up the steps.

Growing up, when I saw this level of seriousness on Tracy's face, I knew there was a problem; a problem that she was gonna solve. She had never been a big girl. Her five-foot-three, one-hundred and twenty-five-pound frame often put people at ease. But, that girl could fight, and she was a bully. It was her way of telling the world 'don't let the light skin and small package fool you.'

Not only was she like this with women, but with men, too. I think she scared most of them away. And for those men who liked a good fight, she combatted them with her tongue. Fighting was her life; the source of her anger was her absentee father.

I didn't let her knock on the door; I opened it before she could. Tracy crossed the threshold, stopped, looked me up and down, and continued walking into the living room. If I couldn't detect her attitude, her rolling eyes and the sound of her heels hitting the floor gave it away. She dropped her keys into her Michael Kors bag. "I'm glad you're alive, but you look terrible."

Tracy gave tough love. The only thing I could do was chuckle. My stained gray sweatpants, mismatched socks and one of Brian's wife beaters, which still smelled like him, hung over my shoulders.

"Thanks, I love you too." Even though she had already walked past me, I held the door open wider and pretended I was inviting her in with an extension of my arm.

She kicked her shoes off, a sign that she wasn't leaving anytime soon. "You know we've been calling and calling. You didn't have to do this alone. A short text would've been nice."

I closed the door. Plopping down on the couch, I tapped the cushion next to me and motioned for Tracy to sit down. I knew by the arch in her eyebrows that she suspected something.

She sat down and reached her arms out to me. "I didn't want to come in here fussing, but we were worried. You know that West Coast friend of yours had been texting and calling me. I played nice because I knew she was your second best friend after me. I told her to give you a few days. But then you weren't taking my calls either."

"What would you say if I told you that I was pregnant?"

If her eyes could, they would've popped out of their sockets. She answered me emphasizing each word. "I'd say that you've been sitting in here trippin'."

Stretching my legs out on the ottoman, I leaned my head back and closed my eyes. When I opened them, Tracy was staring at me.

"You're serious." She asked, but it was more of a statement.

Nervous energy told me to pull the straps of Brian's undershirt up onto my shoulders. I couldn't believe I was discussing this pregnancy with anyone other than him. "Yes, and I'm scared."

Tracy sat up and leaned closer to me. "Did Brian know?"

The memories of that day came flooding back. Through the tears I responded. "He knew. The doctor confirmed it for us that morning."

She knew the morning I was talking about.

Worry lines formed on Tracy's forehead and compassion poured from her eyes. "Oh Chelle, I'm sorry. Why didn't you tell me?"

In the back of my head, I heard Diana Ross singing *Good Morning Heartache*. My mother played that like it was her fight song. They say depression is hereditary, but I'm adopted. I guess spirits didn't concern themselves with DNA.

"I can give you excuse after excuse. But, you know what depression does to me. I just wanted to isolate myself."

The silence that ensued was loud. After a minute Tracy and I were able to discuss the events of July 1, 1993, the day Christian was born...still.

"Lachelle." Tracy knew to whisper in this moment. The fog in my head didn't allow me to open my eyes, but I recognized my best friend's voice.

"Lachelle."

I nodded, this time so she'd know that I wasn't asleep.

"I saw your mother in the hallway."

Translation: I know what happened to the baby.

Fighting sedation, I won the battle. In a blink, my eyes adjusted to the light filtering through the blinds. "Please close them." Sun equated to happiness. There was nothing happy here.

After cooperating, she dragged a chair and pulled it beside my hospital bed. Tracy held my hand and her warmth cascaded through my body.

"Are you in pain?"

Pain. I guess it depended on what kind of pain. I didn't feel anything. I wiggled my toes and moved my fingers; no physical pain. But, how long would I have to get over the emotional pain of not taking my baby home?

A tear rolled down my face. "No, just groggy."

Once I found out that I was pregnant, it took a while before I could wrap my head around having a baby right after I graduated from high school; talk about an unplanned pregnancy. But, as he grew inside of me, so did my love for him.

Tracy loved him, too. She was gonna be his Godmother. She'd purchased his first pair of Jordan's and the cutest little Nike shirt and shorts.

"Who else did you see?" I asked wondering if John possessed some sort of superpower that could transport him here within hours.

"I saw Mrs. Braxton out there huddled up with a nurse, looking like she was signing some papers, talking 'bout, 'you almost messed this up.'"

Almost messed this up. What did that mean?

That's when I felt a punch in my stomach. Was this the pain coming to the surface? Like the sudden burst of a blackhead, tears erupted. They flowed and flowed; Tracy wiped each one.

As the tears flowed down our faces at the memory, Tracy asked, "Can you go through that again?"

I knew what she meant, although she'd never say it. 'Are you sure you should have this baby' was what she was thinking.

Etching my index finger into the dust on the coffee table, I said, "Brian and I had the same discussion, before..."

"You know I'm here for you, regardless of your decision."

"I know, I'm gonna listen to God and see what He tells me to do. I believe that I already know His answer, but I'm in serious listening mode."

"Okay, we'll leave the conversation there for today. But, don't do anything without telling me."

"Never," I told her.

Jumping up to get her bag, Tracy pulled out her Mac. After situating herself on the couch, she opened it up to show me flyers that she started.

"What is it that you Christians say, 'Faith without works is dead,' right?"

"Stop it. You're a Christian."

"Well, I'm not one of those churchy folks, going around talking all holier than thou. If you ask one of the girls in the shop how is she doing, you always get some type of churchy response, 'blessed and highly favored,' 'too blessed to be stressed.' Chica, please."

I couldn't help but contemplate on Tracy's Christian comment. Could you be a Christian and have anger toward God? Did my depression lead to this anger or vice versa? How could God love me and take away my earthly joy?

"Earth to Lachelle," Tracy summoned me out of my head.

"I started these flyers so that we could post them around the area and on social media to help track that fool down."

That hadn't even occurred to me. If she could do it, then I could assist.

"Let's do this. I'm ready to walk back into the world. Let me grab my superwoman cape."

"You don't need it; you have me. Just like always."

Chapter 8

Breathe. Just breathe.

The cameras, the microphones...this was a lot. People called me an introvert. I was quiet, but never shy; they were two different things. While other kids were always loud, and voicing their opinions about what they would and wouldn't do, I kept most of my thoughts in my head. But, when asked to do something that others might feel uncomfortable doing, I stepped up to the plate.

Danielle Banks, a church member and one of the local broadcast journalists, reached out to me about doing an interview, to spread the word that Brian's murderer had not been caught and about the $10,000 reward. Someone knew where he was; helping him to hide.

I sat and watched as the production team staged my living room.

Carrying my favorite vase with both hands, Tracy asked, "Can the flowers fit in here?"

Danielle's assistants brought gorgeous flowers that could only bloom in June. Pictures of Brian and me, Brian and his team, and Brian, alone, were placed behind and beside my chair. They said that we should have the interview here so people would think of Brian the way he lived. They would interview neighbors and of course, talk to a few of the boys who played for Brian.

"Lachelle. Lachelle."

Danielle gently stroked my arm to bring me out of my daze. I turned my focus to her. Danielle Banks was the journalist everyone in D.C. loved. Not only was she pretty, but she was smart. She could interview the mayor and those in the most underserved communities in the city, with respect and compassion.

"How are you feeling?" Danielle's melodic voice snapped me out of my thoughts.

"I'm okay, a little nervous but ready."

Hugging me, she confirmed my thoughts. "You're doing what's best in this situation. You are bringing a personal touch to Brian's story. This plea from you may touch someone's heart to share information that might bring Brian's murderer to justice. Is there anything more you want to share with us? Anything more that you'd like to highlight?"

Well, I could tell the world that I was about six weeks pregnant. How's that for sympathy? But, I wasn't looking for sympathy. I wanted justice.

"No, I think you know everything."

"Okay, let's get you mic'd up."

The production assistant found the best spot for the microphone on my blouse so the audience wouldn't see it.

The director yelled, "Five minutes before taping. Everyone in your places."

Tracy noticed me pulling my earlobe, something I often did when I was nervous. Sitting down next to me, her authoritative voice gave me strength. "You've got this."

I knew I could do it. I had to do it. Just when we were about to begin the interview, there was a knock at the door. I didn't want to move with the microphone on. Tracy looked at me and nodded toward the door, asking if she should open it.

Once Tracy opened it, I heard her before I saw her.

"Tracy," I heard my sister-in-law's greeting. Then her volume increased, and her attitude entered the room before she did. "Gurl, get outta my way. This was my brother's house. I can come in here wheneva I want to."

I knew Tracy wasn't going to take that laying down, company or no company. I asked the production assistant to take my microphone off.

Danielle looked worried.

"I'll be right back. Give me a few minutes, and we can get started."

Danielle's forced smile told me she was worried. Hurrying past the camera crew, I attempted to step in front of Keisha.

Key word: attempted.

When the smell of weed almost knocked me down, I knew this wouldn't go well.

"What's going on here?" Keisha asked as she surveyed the room.

I guess Brian's death wasn't going to change anything. Saying hello to me seemed to kill her. After looking around the room she turned her head to me and stared me down like I owed her an explanation.

After twelve years of marriage, I understood that she had no interest in being my friend. *So why is she here?*

"What y'all doing?" Keisha asked again, still staring while sitting down next to Danielle, crossing her legs like she was an invited guest.

"Why don't you leave, nobody is checking for you," Tracy said as she stepped closer to the love seat.

Talking to Tracy, but focusing on me, she declared, "I ain't going nowhere. You got Brian's insurance money yet? I know he wanted me to have some."

Keisha turned her glance and finally noticed who was sitting next to her. "Ohhh snap, you dat lady that we see on the news all the time."

Extending her hand, Danielle's humbleness filled the room, "Yes, I'm Danielle Banks. How are you?"

Attempting to make this introduction more formal, I stepped in.

"Keisha, this is Danielle Banks a friend and a news reporter for NBC. Danielle, this is Keisha, my sister-in-law."

"Yes, I'm Brian's sister."

Before she could say any more, I continued, "We're taping a segment that will be aired to try to get someone to step up and share any information they may have about the whereabouts of Brian's murderer."

I could tell by the way Keisha's glazed over eyes started moving that she was thinking. I tried to preempt any crazy thoughts from entering her head.

"Keisha, do you mind going into the den while we do the interview? It won't take long. We can talk after it's over."

"I should be in the interview, too. I can talk 'bout Ma and how this has broken her heart. I know you have something that I can put on."

"Gurl, don't nobody want your stank…"

"Tracy!" I yelled not only with my voice but with my eyes.

"Who you calling stank? I know your track record? You ain't no better than me," Keisha shot back, jumping up out of the love seat. In one motion she was in Tracy's face. No one moved, but everyone's eyes followed her.

At this point, I knew the interview wasn't going to happen today. Keisha wasn't going anywhere, and the crew had to be someplace else, soon. Danielle had squeezed us into her schedule.

Tracy, with her hands on her hips and head cocked to the side, begged Keisha to hit her, without saying one word.

"Tracy and Keisha, please let me talk to Danielle for a minute. Can you both go into the den?"

Neither of them moved. If they were in the street, a smackdown would've already ensued. They knew better in my house.

"Please y'all, just let me talk to Danielle for a minute."

Tracy moved first, stepping to the side so Keisha could go past. Keisha whipped her weave and stomped into the den.

Exhaling then sitting down next to Danielle, I said, "I don't think today will be a good day to do this. I appreciate you for encouraging me."

"We will do this. I'll call you in a few days to set something up."

We hugged, and I watched as the camera crew packed everything up. I wondered if they were packing up hope of catching Brian's murderer, too.

Tracy led Keisha from the den after she heard the door close.

"Oh, your company left?" Keisha's sarcasm fell on deaf ears. I decided not to say anything to her because it wouldn't have been nice.

As I walked to the staircase that led to my bedroom, I spoke to Tracy. "I'm going upstairs to chill for little while. Tracy please lock the door after Keisha leaves."

"Oh! I've been put out of better places."

Whatever.

Tracy stayed the night at my house. She fell asleep in the living room watching Real Housewives reruns, all franchises. Not me, though. Leaving Tracy in the living room, I put our popcorn bowls into the sink and tip-toed up the steps to my bedroom, careful not to wake her. I hurried to my closet where I hid Brian's pillow. It smelled so much like his cologne, still. I hid it so neither Tracy nor Vanessa would wash it, stripping me of Brian's scent.

After stepping out of my sweats, I climbed into the bed. My body extended into a long stretch before curling up in a fetal position with Brian's pillow. I inhaled as much of him as I could. The only light in the room was the red numbers on the clock screaming 12:40 and tomorrow was my first day back to work. I needed to sleep. After I pulled the covers back on his side of the bed, I rolled over and tucked myself in. Sirens cut through the peace of the night. Then there was silence…and Brian.

He was at that grill in the backyard flipping hamburgers. I ran to him, but with every step I took, he moved farther away. Then he was coaching his team. The faster I ran down the bleachers toward the football field, the farther away he moved. Then he was outside of Ben's and this time; I ran out of the door. Again, as I ran toward him, the scene moved farther away. Then there was a boom. It caused me to shoot straight up in my bed, but reaching for Brian just like I was in my dream.

Would this ever end? Maybe I needed to read some scriptures. My Bible stayed inside of the top drawer of my nightstand. I turned to reach for the handle and slid the drawer open. I pulled it out and flipped the pages hoping a scripture would jump out at me. Nothing did. I couldn't believe that God would do this to me, taking the love of my life away from me. One minute I was happy, looking forward to the future and the next minute I was questioning what kind of future I would have without Brian.

I'd never felt this alone and separated from God in my life, not even after Christian died. Maybe I was destined to be alone; no Christian, no Brian and no God.

I threw the Bible at the foot of my bed. My chest heaved up and down as I moaned and cried into Brian's pillow. After what seemed like an hour, my eyes commanded my body to sleep because there were no more tears to cry.

Chapter 9

The June rain tapping against the window greeted me as I walked into my office. It has been two weeks since Brian was murdered. It was time to go back to work. I needed my paycheck. Like Keisha, people thought because of the reward money posted, that I had received a windfall of insurance money. Not. We didn't prepare very well for an unexpected tragedy. As a teacher and coach, Brian didn't make a lot of money, but we made the most of what we had. Working for a non-profit organization had its ups and downs. Most times we got our checks, sometimes we didn't. When we didn't, we'd have to wait for funding to come in from various grants and that was rough. Health insurance was expensive through my organization. I thanked God for Obamacare. It paid for everything associated with my pregnancy.

When I stood in my office, everything looked the same, but nothing was the same. The pictures of Brian and I were situated on my desk and on the bookstands. Rain was the appropriate backdrop.

I'd decided to arrive early to prevent anyone from seeing me if I broke down. And if I did, I'd just turn around and try it another day. I'd told my supervisor that I'd come in one day this week; I didn't give her an exact date. Thankfully, she understood and didn't press me for one.

Before the spirit of depression was able to put a noose around my neck, the aroma of strong, black coffee whirled around my nose. I wasn't alone. The only one who made the office coffee was Janis, the lead of our administrative support team. Others would name that job a secretary, but our Executive Director wanted everyone in the organization to know they were a part of the mission of *Loving Our Babies.* So our organization was broken into various teams, and administrative support was our backbone.

"Coffee or tea this morning?"

I dropped the cloth that I'd been using to dust the bookshelf. Although I knew someone was here, Janis' voice startled me back from my thoughts.

"I am so sorry. I should've ring your phone before I came around."

"Gurl, come on in," I told her as we walked toward each other.

Her embrace was warm. She allowed me to rest my head on her shoulder and breathe. How did she know that I needed that kind of hug? That was Janis for you. She gave everyone what they needed without having to ask.

"Sit down, my friend," I said, waving my arm toward the chair in front of my desk.

Setting the two cups on the desk, she asked again, "Coffee or tea?"

"I'll take the tea. Why are you here at seven-thirty?"

After taking a sip of what smelled like black coffee from her Wonder Woman mug, Janis said, "Cynthia told me you might come in today. And I know you. If you say, you might do something that is just like saying you will. You follow through on everything. I wanted to see how you were doing before everyone came in and the day started; just like we're doing now."

It was good to have an office friend. I mean, someone who had your back at work that you could trust, who would look out for you, holistically.

"And you know, I plan to keep folks out of here so that you can ease back into the office slowly. Some of us don't know what to say to people, and some are just downright messy."

Yep. We had some messy ninjas in our office on regular issues. Brian's death was major, so I understood exactly where she was coming from.

We talked about the progress of my cases, and of course, she gave me the tea on office gossip. I didn't mention the pregnancy, although, when I figured this thing out, she would be one of the next in my life to know.

"Thank you, lady; I needed this four-one-one. Uhmmm, you look like that dress is hanging off of you."

Janis had battled weight issues for the entire seven years I had known her. I wanted to compliment her on her weight loss. I knew that our relationship dictated that I could.

"Chile! I've been drinking these green smoothies. I didn't think I had the willpower to do it, but I've been doing them for a few weeks now. When I'm not drinking them for my three meals, I drink one in the morning, and I eat healthy meals for lunch and dinner with small healthy snacks throughout the day. I started going to aqua-fitness classes, too."

"You go, girl! I love it. I should join you for those aqua-fitness classes."

"I'll send you the information before the day is over," she said as she looked at her watch. "Oh, let me get over to my desk before folks start coming in."

"You know I'm glad we had a few minutes before the day started. Our talk has given me the umph I needed to get started."

Before walking out the door, Janis turned and said, "Don't stay all day if you don't feel like it. I didn't put anyone on your calendar. Don't. Feel. Pressured."

I smiled and mouthed, "Thank you."

Music seemed to be in order. Grabbing my cell phone off the desk, I scrolled the playlist. Music would certainly help me get through the barrage of emails that stared me in my face after turning on the computer. I stopped at contemporary gospel, upbeat music. Searching the playlist, I prayed, "Lord speak to me."

Immediately, Fred Hammond's bass guitar filled the room, and I heard his background singers asking me, "Are you ready for your blessing? Are you ready for your miracle?"

Let the Praise Begin. Brian and I used to jam off this. He'd pretend to play the bass like a pro, and I'd sing like one of the background singers.

Okay, Lord. I hear you.

"It's in your praise. It's in your praise," Fred's background singers seemed to scream at me.

Would it be in my praise? Would I find joy in my praise? Would I find peace of mind in my praise? Would Brian come back in my praise? The dreams, or should I say nightmares, of Brian and I trying to reach each other, but once we got ready to touch, he'd disappear, were horrendous. What I wouldn't give to talk to him one more time.

While in my thoughts, I heard a light tap on the door. "Come on in."

Janis stuck her head in. "Sherry called in sick today. We weren't able to contact her first appointment in time."

The worry on her face told me what she needed. She didn't have to ask. "I'll take her. But I need her..."

Before I could finish my sentence, Janis slid the client's folder on my desk.

As the morning rain gave way to the sun, I flipped through the file for Shanita Jones, a young mom pregnant with her second child. Many of our clients came here because they didn't have insurance to go to an HMO.

I walked into the waiting area and greeted Ms. Jones. She was alone. She told me that she dropped her youngest off at school before coming into the office.

As we sat down, I noticed her looking at everything in the office, taking in the pictures especially. I decided to start the conversation before she asked about Brian.

"Do you want any water or anything? Are you comfortable?"

Crossing her legs and sitting back in the chair, she told me she had some water while she was waiting and that she felt fine.

"I see you are about four months pregnant and this is your third time coming into the office."

"Yes, I hope Mrs. Brady is okay. I probably just missed her call."

"She's just a little under the weather. But Sherry keeps her files in perfect order, so we have everything we need, right here," I said as I held up her folder. "I see that you are up-to-date with all of the appointments we've scheduled for you."

"Yes, I'm excited. The pregnancy was a surprise. I felt overwhelmed initially. People say 'aren't you too young to have two kids and you ain't married?' But I go to church, and I know that God wouldn't give us more than we can bear. My pastor says that all the time."

Wow! This young lady was preaching to me, and she didn't even know it.

As she pulled out her phone to show me pictures of her three-year-old son, she continued. "My son is my joy. Watching him helps put the hard times out of my mind. He's the reason I get up every morning. I love my stinka boo."

I sat there dumbfounded at first. Yes, I was scared my baby might cause me my life. Yes, I was scared that raising a baby alone was never in my plan. But, as I sat, I could only admire Shanita and see myself in her.

I responded with, "And you *should* love that stinka. He is too cute. I won't keep you longer than I have to. We've enrolled you in your parenting classes, and you decided that you want to deliver here."

"Yes, I would like to do the water birth, and they don't offer that at the hospital. I've read so much about it."

"Women love it."

"And I know that it is never too late to learn better parenting skills."

"Never."

"So I'm done?"

"You. Are. Done. Thank you for coming in early this morning. I'll update your file and talk to Mrs. Brady. But, feel free to schedule your next appointment before you leave with Janis."

After I walked her out to the waiting area, I returned to my office and sat down. The joy in her eyes, I couldn't get my mind off it. I felt a little lighter; the depression that gnawed at me seemed to loosen its grip.

After spending time with Shanita, I knew where I'd go for lunch. I knew who I had to talk to, as I hadn't spoken to her in a few weeks. It was time for me to go and talk to First Lady Kendra Smith. She'd help me sort through the conflict that weighed on my heart.

Chapter 10

I stopped at the smoothie shop on Georgia Avenue, a few blocks north of Howard University, before visiting Lady Kendra. I called the church earlier, and they told me I could come by during lunch. Lady Kendra loved her healthy snacks, and I wanted to surprise her.

Greeting me with a hug, Lady Kendra appeared in the waiting area outside of her office, looking as though she was fresh out of a yoga class, wearing the cutest tennis shoes.

"Is one of those green concoctions for me?"

"Of course. I knew that you loved them."

"I'm so glad that you called today. You know you've been in our prayers."

Pastor Smith and Lady Kendra were a dynamic duo. His preaching style was more teaching that resonated with the congregation. Lady Kendra's work ethic and graciousness pulled people to her like a magnet.

"Yes, and I'm sorry that I haven't been returning your calls."

Lady Kendra had called me a few times, and I felt like a sinner because I didn't call her back. Who did that? Knowing how busy she stayed with the church and that she took time from her schedule to personally call me. I was guilty.

Fanning her hand, she said, "Don't worry about that. I know that the last few weeks have been hard. I'm glad God led you here so that we could connect."

"It has been hard. There were days when I couldn't get out of bed. There were days when I heard Brian's voice. But most of all, it has been the guilt..." Letting out an exasperated sigh, I reached for a tissue and continued, "The guilt of being mad at God. It seems that for the second time in my life, He took love away from me. I've felt so guilty about my questions, especially when I asked Him if He doesn't want anyone to love me?"

Reaching across the desk for my hands, she reassured me, "I counsel many people going through the same type of situation and who have the same questions."

Lady Kendra stood to pull her Bible from the bookcase. She sat back down, flipped the pages, and took a sip of her smoothie. She nodded and smiled upon landing on the scripture that she wanted to share. "Let's read this scripture together; John four and twenty-four."

She rose to come to the other side of the desk to make reading together more comfortable.

In unison, we read, "God is Spirit, and those who worship Him must worship in spirit and truth."

What did this have to do with my issues?

As if reading my mind, she said, "Sugah, don't beat yourself up for the way you feel. The fact that you even feel uncomfortable with those thoughts is a good thing. But, what I want you to walk away with today is that we worship God in spirit and truth, not spirit and perfection."

She let that sink in for a moment before adding, "You are not perfect, none of us are. Take things day by day. Sometimes you'll take a few steps forward and then take more backward. Allow yourself to go through the process."

I was not perfect, and I'd been beating myself up as though I was.

"You'll feel God's peace as you go through the process. I'm not saying that it will be easy."

The church secretary buzzed the phone to let Lady Kendra know that it was time for her next meeting. I rose to leave, but she shook her head, motioning me to stay seated.

Once she hung up, she told me, "We aren't done. I wanted to talk a little more."

"I plan to go back to work. I feel better, and you will see me more. I'll try to come back, slowly. But I don't want to keep you any longer."

Before I left, we prayed. I knew that Lady Kendra's office was a safe space. The Word, the Word, I was going to keep focused on the Word.

Chapter 11

It had been twenty-four days, five hundred and seventy-six hours and thirty-four thousand, five hundred and sixty minutes since Brian died. D.C.'s summer humidity decided to visit us earlier in the season this year; evidenced by the puffiness of my hair. The puffiness of my eyes, now that was another story.

I didn't get any sleep last night. I tossed and turned until I thought about my meeting with Lady Kendra a week before. *Stay focused on His Word.* I opened the Bible and started reading, this time. I woke up with it lying on my chest, the sun greeting me as if saying hello. Birds hovered outside of my window and their melodies added to the beauty of the morning.

After washing up, I fixed toast and made a cup of tea, adding honey to it. It was Saturday, and I didn't have any place to go, so I decided to take my Bible on the front porch and eat my breakfast. Brian had installed a ceiling fan on our porch a few years ago. Memories of us sitting out here as the sun rose surprisedly felt good. As I sat down and put my feet on the ottoman, I noticed an Uber driver looking at the addresses on each of the houses. Then I saw Vanessa pointing to our house.

What is she doing here? She hadn't even told me she was coming. My soror, my line sister, my girl; of course she'd come back. We were roommates all four years in college. Vanessa and I shared that journey and had not parted ways since.

I stood up so that I could see if it was really her.

The Uber driver drove past my house and backed up to a screeching halt when he identified my house numbers. Vanessa jumped out of the back of the car, followed by the driver.

He popped the trunk, trying to get her bags out for her, but Vanessa shoved him to the side, "I'll get them myself. You almost gave me whiplash."

"Ohhhh, I'm giving him the worst rating possible," she said as she walked up the four steps, onto the porch.

"What are you doing here? Why didn't you call me?"

Throwing my words back in my face, she asked, "Why didn't I call you? Really? I can't believe you're asking that."

I ignored her remark, grabbed one of her bags and asked, "How long will you be here? I mean you know you're always welcome, I was just wondering with these two big bags."

Putting her empty arm around me, she said, "As long as I need to."

We went into the house and took Vanessa's things to the spare bedroom. It'd been two weeks since Vanessa was here. "After you get settled, come on downstairs, and we can talk."

Now would be a good time to tell her about the baby. If I waited any longer, she'd kill me. Her feelings would be hurt that she wasn't one of the first to know.

I went into the kitchen to see what was in there that someone other than me would even think about eating.

I heard Vanessa coming down the steps and I turned to face her with a sad face, as there really wasn't much to eat.

"Why the look?" Vanessa eased out of her shoes, grabbed her phone from her pocket and plopped down onto the bar stool in front of the kitchen nook.

"I wanted to fix you some food, but I don't see anything in here to eat."

"I thought D.C. had turned into a," using air quotes she finished her sentence, "walkable community."

After I thought about it, I remembered that a quaint restaurant serving breakfast and lunch only had popped up a few blocks away on Rhode Island Avenue. I thought we'd try it.

As we walked to get breakfast, Vanessa told me about her latest adventure in skydiving. I was excited for her until she gave me the entire story.

"I noticed a cute guy on Facebook whose profile pic was of him skydiving. So I thought that if I created a profile picture of me skydiving, I'd get his attention."

I couldn't help myself; I literally stopped on the sidewalk. A biker was coming, so it was perfect timing. As Vanessa tried to continue walking, I grabbed her arm. "You did what, for what?"

"Uhm, yeah. I thought it was a good idea. It didn't work, but it could've. Guys want women who are adventurous. The picture didn't attract him, but it may attract someone else."

I loved my line sister. But, sometimes I heard Tracy's voice in my head, *She ain't wrapped too tight.*

Vanessa continued, "Don't think that I'm not praying about it. Don't think that I don't trust God with this. But, you know the scripture says, 'Faith without works is dead.' I'm just putting in my work."

Vanessa's description of how she intended to meet her Mr. Right brought back memories of how Brian and I met.

We met at a Mayor Marion Barry's Youth Leadership Institute Alumni Conference. I was a participant in the leadership program while in high school. I returned to the annual conference to serve as a workshop facilitator. Brian accompanied a few of his players to the conference. Our eyes met, and the rest was history.

Vanessa and I bought our breakfast, walked back to the house, ate and then, I curled up on the couch, and Vanessa pulled one of my throw blankets from the closet and fell asleep in the lounge chair. When we woke up, I knew that I couldn't put it off any longer.

"When are you going to tell me the entire reason for your visit?" I asked because I knew Vanessa; she just didn't come to check on me. She might've needed some time away from L.A., and I wanted to find out if my suspicions were correct.

"Well...you know I thought I landed a role-playing Taraji's sister in a movie that is supposed to come out next year, right?"

"Yeah, I remember. That's why you left right after Brian's...services."

Vanessa reached down to the floor and grabbed her purse. She pulled out her cell phone and showed me the picture of a man's Facebook page. Although he was an older gentleman, he didn't look too bad.

"Who is he?" I asked.

"He is the producer of the movie who kept making sexual advances toward me to solidify that I had the part." The glimmer in her eyes dimmed, and her upbeat personality took a downturn. "That joker would not leave me alone."

"Did he..?"

"No, he never raped me. But, if we were left alone, I think he would've tried. I had my agent call and remove my name from consideration."

A tear dropped from her eye which turned into a tsunami. Vanessa had been trying to get into A-list movies since we graduated and she moved home to L.A. She landed a few small roles but they didn't pay the rent. Since she was a trained dancer, she taught youth how to dance and created a hip-hop dance group for kids.

"I'll get some wine," I told her. Once we sorted through her pain, I'd reveal mine. I pushed myself up off the couch and walked into the kitchen. I grabbed two wine glasses, a bottle of wine and a can of Sprite. By the time I returned, Vanessa's tears had turned into a light drizzle.

Vanessa grabbed the remote control, turned the TV on and surfed the channels. I didn't think that my Sprite would capture her attention. The glasses clicked as I put them on the coffee table, causing Vanessa to turn her head to the direction of the sound. "Why are you drinking Sprite? I don't want to drink alone."

"Wait, I want to hear more about this scumbag who tried to take advantage of you."

"I'm good. It hurts me to my core that some men use their power to take advantage of women. Fortunately, I resisted. But, the casting couch is real. I refused to be a part of that in Hollywood. Now tell me, why are you drinking Sprite?"

I uncorked the bottle and poured Vanessa's wine, before handing her the glass. I waited until she took a sip before I announced, "Line sister, I'm eight weeks pregnant."

Vanessa's shock exposed itself as she almost gagged on her first sip. "I'd better put this down and listen. On second thought let me get another sip before you continue."

Vanessa knew my medical history, so I didn't have to explain my concern. Instead, she wanted to know how I was coping and whether Brian knew or not. Then she asked the question that I kept putting out of my mind. "Do you see this as God's way of giving you a piece of Brian?"

"I've thought about that, but I'm not sure if this is a blessing or a curse. I'm just getting used to Brian not being here. Going through a pregnancy alone and possibly being sick on top of that. Gurl…"

"Just remember that God may have ordained the pregnancy so that you wouldn't be alone. Let's try to look at this as a blessing. Babies are not a curse."

Vanessa was always an idealist. I was a realist. But, deep in the innermost part of me, I knew she was right.

"You now know everything, my dear sistah. The one thing that I haven't been able to do is to begin packing some of Brian's things. I hadn't thought about packing anything, but the library up the street is looking for donated books and Brian had a ton of them. Since you're here, can you help me get started?"

"I'm here with you; whatever you need."

We walked into the den and started with Brian's books. His Bible sat on his desk directly in front of the chair.

"He might've been sitting here reading before…"

"You're right," I told her. "He was in here most of the weekend before he passed. I was in bed most of that weekend."

I picked it up, closed my eyes and held it to my chest. I'd given this Bible to Brian for his birthday, two years previously. It was one of his favorites, The Men of Color Study Bible. It would be something that I'd pack up last. Before I put the book back on the desk, a piece of paper fell out, landing on Vanessa's foot. She picked it up and handed it to me, without reading it.

I almost fell when I read the note. Was Brian speaking to me from the grave?

After reading the note, I didn't doubt what I needed to do next.

Chapter 12

I was fortunate that Dr. Price had an appointment available. For the whole week, I still hadn't answered the question if Brian was speaking to me from the grave or not. Sitting in the office looking at Brian's note, his scribble was hard to read, but it was clear. There were two columns, one with the heading Boys and the other, Girls. The list of the boys' names was long, but it appeared that he'd settled on Brian Joseph Jackson, Jr. That was the only name that didn't have a line crossed through it. There were no names in the girls' column but instead, a question mark.

I told Brian that I was pregnant on a Thursday and he died the next Monday, so I was sure that he wrote this list the weekend before he died and he probably thought he had time to get back to it.

I still wasn't sure if Brian was speaking to me, but after reading the note, I knew that God was with me, giving me everything I needed when I needed it. A sense of peace began to fill the sadness dwelling in my heart.

"Mrs. Jackson." Dr. Price greeted me with a warm hug, bringing me out of my daze. "I know the last three weeks have been rough."

I took a deep breath, forcing a smile.

She continued. "I'm glad that you came in. Based on the tests, you are eight weeks pregnant. How have you been feeling?"

I thought about it for the first time. "I've been feeling okay, physically. Of course, I've been depressed, not wanting to get out of bed, not wanting to eat. But, one of my best friends is in town, and she's been helping me."

"So, no morning sickness?"

"Nope."

"Great. If you want to have the baby, we can discuss the details of the plans that I discussed earlier." She let a beat go by. "And if you don't..." She looked directly at me. "We'll talk again next week. How does that sound?"

I knew what she was saying. But I knew what I came to tell her. "Dr. Price, I'm going to keep my baby."

The brightness of her smile was her approval.

I continued. "And I'll follow your instructions."

She nodded her approval and agreement.

"Can you tell me more about symptoms to look for and strategies that we might use to ensure that we stay healthy?"

Dr. Price went back into doctor mode, hands folded on her desk. "Absolutely. Do you remember I mentioned before that your pregnancy is high-risk by default because you're over thirty-five?"

At forty-two, I didn't anticipate getting pregnant. I nodded to let her know that I was following along.

"You will continue to see me, as your primary OB/GYN. You will also see a perinatologist."

I was sure my face twisted when she said the last word.

Dr. Price smiled. "Perinatologists specialize in high-risk pregnancies. We work together to do our best to make sure that you and the baby get the best care."

Continuing, she told me, "Signs or symptoms of preeclampsia are swelling, rapid weight gain, very bad headaches or dizziness. This usually happens closer to the end of the pregnancy, but I want you to be vigilant. Don't hesitate to call us if you experience those symptoms or anything else that makes you feel uncomfortable."

Knowing that I'd have two doctors looking after me was a comfort.

"There is one more thing that we might consider," she said as I was just feeling a little lighter.

"We may consider delivering the baby a few weeks before your due date. We'd want to ensure that the baby has developed enough; the closer the birth to your due date, the better for our little one."

If I counted correctly, I would be due in January. I might even have a Christmas bundle of joy. At that moment I felt that I was moving forward. Then I remembered there was one thing that I promised Brian that I'd do. He'd promised to do it with me. I knew he'd be with me in spirit. But, I was blessed because I had both of my girls in town to get me through the pilgrimage that I promised Brian I'd take. He said it would help alleviate the pain and the grief. I was ready to see if Brian's prediction was correct.

Chapter 13

On what would've been Christian's twenty-third birthday, I woke up to a rumbling stomach. When I felt last night's dinner abruptly rising, my feet couldn't hit the floor fast enough. Morning sickness greeted me like an avalanche blowing down my bedroom door. I threw the covers back and ran toward the bathroom on the other side of the bed. My knees and my head assumed the position in front of the toilet. I saw food from last night and then green stuff, as my body convulsed. I obeyed its command because the sooner it was out the sooner it would be over.

It finally stopped. With tears in my eyes, I sat on the edge of the tub for a few minutes to compose myself, trying to steady my breathing. I hoped this morning sickness thing didn't last long. I wasn't so sure if it was morning sickness or if I was nervous about going to visit Christian. My hands trembled as I pulled myself up using the side of the bathtub to rise and remembered my conversation with Tracy.

When I told Tracy that I wanted her to go with me to visit Christian, she didn't fuss. I expected her to rant and rave about leaving the *past in the past*. Her response surprised me. "His birthday is next week. Why don't we go then?"

Really! Tracy remembered Christian's birthday, July 1st. Blood didn't make us sisters, life's journeys did; innocence lost, maturity gained. She knew that I coped with this by tucking it away in the recesses of my mind and she'd respected that.

After I dressed, I went to the kitchen. Tracy and Vanessa were waiting for me, ready to go.

"Good morning Sunshine." Vanessa greeted me in a sarcastic tone because I didn't look anything like the sun.

I grabbed a barstool and sat down at the breakfast nook. Tracy flipped a huge pancake. "That wasn't for me, was it? I just threw up everything I've eaten over the last year. I know I did."

"Well Chica, it was. I'll fix you some toast and tea because you should try to put something on your stomach. I'll wrap it, and you can take it with you."

No sympathy here. *No excuses* was Tracy's look to me.

"You guys go ahead to the car. Give me a few minutes to lock up."

Tracy gave me the look. *Don't play with me.*

I gave her my look and responded. "I'm coming, just give me a few minutes."

They grabbed their purses and walked out of the door.

I looked into the huge, silver trimmed mirror hanging by the door and smoothed my hair. After I applied my lipstick, a smile stretched across my face. Tracy and Vanessa were going with me, but I knew that Brian was right beside me, just like he promised.

I locked the door and got into the back of Tracy's Mercedes Benz C350.

If you were from D.C., you'd probably bury your loved one in one of three cemeteries. Christian was buried at National Harmony Memorial Park, right across the D.C. line in Landover, MD. The air conditioner was on full blast while WHUR, Howard University's radio station, played a few hip-hop hits from the 90's. Bell, Biv, DeVoe's Poison blasted, followed by Wreckx-n-Effect's Rump Shaker.

"Yup yup it's Teddy, ready with the one-two checker. Wreckx-n-effect is in effects, but I'm the Wrecker."

Tracy looked into the rearview mirror to make sure I was okay. She couldn't see my eyes because of the sunglasses, so I gave her a thumbs up, and she nodded.

Was I okay? Was this really a journey that I needed to travel? I'd know in a few minutes as the cemetery was only fifteen minutes from my house.

"Lachelle, are you sleep? Wake up, we're here," Vanessa's voice echoed through the car.

I wasn't asleep, just resting my eyes, as the seniors say. When I opened them, we were riding between two huge, brick walls. The black granite sign confirmed that we had arrived at the National Harmony Memorial Park Cemetery.

Anxiety replaced peace, and my stomach felt like someone was squeezing it into a knot as we entered. The driveway was smooth as butter, a stark contrast to many of the streets in the metropolitan area.

Trees, with the greenest of green leaves, greeted us as we entered the cemetery. After riding about fifty feet we slowed down at a circle; we could either go left or right.

"Uhm, which way should I go?" Tracy thought out loud.

"Make a left," Vanessa responded. Tracy made a right.

Under different circumstances, I would've burst out laughing.

After Tracy drove to the right, we saw a sign pointing to the office to get the location of Christian's plot.

"Just like you always bet on black, you always go right if you don't know the direction, because it is the *right* way.

Vanessa responded with a *whateva* look in her eyes.

After we got the directions, Tracy drove through the twists and turns of the cemetery, and I placed my hand on my stomach hoping that the tea and toast I was able to eat stayed in place.

"Based on the numbers of the plots, we're here," Vanessa announced. "I'll pull over." Tracy said.

All three of us opened our doors, and I told them, "I know y'all got my back, but I want to walk over there alone and just sit for a while."

"Since we can see you, I'm good with that," Tracy said, giving me her permission.

"You won't be alone. I see someone else over there visiting a loved one, too." Vanessa was right. In the distance, we saw a man sitting in the grass. I hoped there would be a bit of distance between us so that I could let my feelings out in private.

Vanessa gave me the paper with the plot number, and I grabbed the little blue teddy bear I wanted to leave Christian. She gave me tissues, too.

I made my way through the various plots, looking at the names and numbers. It was quiet, except for the birds chirping in the background.

When it seemed that I was getting closer to Christian's, it was clear the man was sitting very close to where I was headed. His back was to me so I couldn't make out his face. The man wasn't moving. Then I saw those long legs stretched out, as he leaned against a small bench under a hibiscus tree with a child-sized basketball sitting next to him. I couldn't believe it. His caramel colored skin; and his older looking baby face, after all of these years.

As he heard the crinkle of a leaf under my foot, he turned around.

"John Braxton?" I was able to say, although very surprised that his name even came out of my mouth.

"What's up, shawty?" he said, standing up.

I hadn't seen him since the night before he left for the University of Kentucky in the summer of 1993.

With his eyes closed, his head dropped. After a few silent moments, he raised his head, and stood up. The pain in his eyes greeted mine.

As we stood there quiet, not knowing what to say, my mind took me back to a time John and I had shared. John had tried to be attentive to me in the spring of our senior year of high school. I didn't want to go to my prom seven months pregnant, so we went to the movies and IHOP instead.

Once we graduated, the demands of recruitment to the University of Kentucky pulled John away. He checked in as often as he could and promised to come back a week before the baby was due in August. But nature happened, and John wasn't my focus once I got sick and delivered early.

Bringing me out of my thoughts, John said, "I've visited him since what would've been his fifth birthday, on this day, every year."

He wiped off the bench and motioned for me to sit down.

"I'm sorry about your husband. Based on everything that I read in the newspaper or heard on the news, he seemed like a good dude."

"He was the best." Then I asked, "How do you know so much about what's going on here?"

I knew that John completed college on his basketball scholarship, then had gone on to the NBA. But after ten years, he'd been cut from Milwaukee. After leaving the NBA, he spent the majority of his basketball career playing for teams in Europe.

"My moms tells me about what's going on here with my friends."

Friends.

"Uhm, your mother. Why would she tell you anything about me? She never liked me."

"Naw, it wasn't that. She didn't want my career to get off track."

I gave him a side-eye as if to ask, *what about me?* He understood and elaborated.

"The spring of our senior year was a trip; coaches from schools visiting us, coming to talk to Coach. Do you remember how many times I had to take the SAT just to make sure that I scored high enough to get into the top schools?"

"But since I didn't have a father, I intended to be there for our baby and for you. But once we graduated." He paused and shook his head. "I didn't have a choice but to leave for summer school to take a few credits so that I wouldn't have to take as many during the year. Part of me wanted to stay here with you, but the other part knew how much my moms had sacrificed the last twelve years of her life to make sure that I had the best. She wanted our dream of the NBA to come true, and I wanted it for her and for me. I had hoped that it would be for us one day. I made my mother promise me that she would step in and do what I would do, be there for you until I could get back home. She knew that not knowing what was going on with you was stressful. I should've called you more often after I left, but you know how it was before we had cell phones. You weren't due until August, and I guess that date was on my mind. Moms didn't even tell me that you got sick and had the baby, prematurely, until at least a week after it happened."

I guess more for him than for me; he repeated, "I didn't even know my son was born until a week afterward. Moms was like, 'they've already buried the baby, so there is no need to come home.' When I didn't hear from you, I took it as a hint that you wanted to move on with your life."

"It happened so quickly," I offered.

"Yeah, but that's no excuse on my part. I called you when my mother finally told me. But, I don't think your mother wanted us to talk either. She kept telling me that I had just missed you or that you were resting."

I chuckled in disbelief. I'd asked my mother if I missed any calls from John. I even checked the mail for letters. I would find cute little notes from John in my spiral notebooks when we first started hanging out. I thought he might've resorted to mail. Then weeks turned into months and months turned to years.

John continued, "Once I graduated from Kentucky, I heard you got married. I didn't want to become a distraction, so I admired you from afar." Then he added, "And I never forgot our little man."

I didn't want John to beat himself up because things worked out the way God intended. "We shared the bond of our baby, but we were young. We weren't in love."

Turning to look him in his eyes I continued. "Yes, we liked each other, and I knew that you would've stood by our baby and me. But, once we lost him I felt like it provided us with the freedom to do what we wanted to do in life. You were destined to play in the NBA, and I was destined for college."

I also felt the need to confess that I hadn't been as loyal to our little man as he had.

"This is my first time here since the day we buried him. Brian suggested that I come. We were planning to come together until..."

Dabbing my face with the tissue, I continued. "Tracy suggested that I come today. Wait...did she know that you were coming here today?"

"Tracy and I are Facebook friends. I use social media as therapy sometimes; I probably said too much on there. Tracy probably figured that I'd be here."

We both laughed.

Then, it hit me. The reward money. I knew I didn't have any friends who could afford to put up that type of money. If it had been any groups that Brian was affiliated with, they would've told me.

I had to know, I had to ask John if it were him especially since he mentioned hearing about Brian's murder and connecting Brian to me.

"Someone anonymously put up a ten thousand dollar reward for information leading to a conviction in Brian's case." I paused and gave him a long stare. "Do you know anything about that?"

"Lachelle, I always cared about you. You were the mother of my first child. You hold a special place in my heart. I'd do anything so you could have a sense of closure."

Brian was my true love; my soulmate. I held no malice in my heart against John. Both of us did the best we could.

Wiping my head with one of my tissues, I said, "This wasn't what I expected when I came here today. I wanted to talk to Christian for a few minutes. There's just a lot of stuff on my mind."

The look on John's face was priceless as he punctuated each word of his next question, probably thinking delivered that way, would produce a positive response from me. "How would you feel if I told Tracy and your other friend that I'll take you home and we can talk in the car? I want you to have time alone here, too. It's hot as fire, and maybe we could stop and get some ice cream or something cool to drink to catch up."

I hadn't seen John in what seemed like one hundred years. But, he was a good dude, and I still trusted him.

"They won't listen to you. I'll text Tracy. My cell phone is in my pocket, but when you go back to your car, please get my purse out of Tracy's and put it in yours."

"I gotchu."

I watched as John walked to the cars, conscious of not walking on anyone's markers. He seemed to zig-zag back to the curb. The text to Tracy took a second and then I focused on my baby.

I sat down on the ground in front of the Christian's marker, smoothing the dirt away, my legs extended with my arms behind me propping me up. "Hey, honey. It's mommy." Twenty-three years earlier, he knew my voice. He'd kick or move at the sound. But, I felt a need to identify myself. "I'm sorry that I haven't been to visit you. You'd be a grown man now." I took a few minutes to imagine him as an adult. Would he have been a basketball player like his father or a doctor, or a lawyer?

"You'll have a brother or a sister soon. And when they are old enough to understand, I'll tell them about my first baby." As a single tear dropped, I was able to whisper, "I love you Christian and I always will." After sitting the teddy bear on his marker, I promised, "I'll be back."

This time I smoothed over the corner of his marker but more in the way that a mother would wipe the corner of her child's mouth or smooth down their hair with a dab of spit from the tip of her finger.

Walking to the car, I saw John, Tracy, and Vanessa. John was leaning against his Cadillac Escalade. Tracy and Vanessa sat in the air-conditioned car. Their doors opened once they saw me and got out.

Vanessa hugged me and asked, "Are you okay?"

I returned her hug longer than I thought I would. "This was good. I'll be back sooner than later."

"Are you sure you want us to leave you?" Vanessa asked while still hugging me so that no one could hear, sounding concerned.

As if he had bionic ears, John responded, "You all don't have to worry. Lachelle is in good hands with me. I'll deliver her back home safe and sound."

Tracy jumped in. "Ain't nobody worried about you. But, you know she's my girl, and I wanted to see her before I left."

"Thank you for waiting, you know I appreciate it. But, we're gonna stop and get a quick snack. We won't be long."

John interjected. "And she'll tell you everything when she gets back."

Tracy punched his arm. "Okay, we're gone." She hugged me, and they both climbed back into the car.

After they drove off, John and I leaned against his truck dazing into the distance at Christian's plot.

"You ready?" I asked.

"Yep, let's get out of the heat. Where do you want to go?" As John opened the door for me, my phone rang. I didn't recognize the number but answered anyway.

"Mrs. Jackson, this is Detective Smith from the Fifth District Police Station. We wanted to let you know that we have apprehended the suspect in your husband's case. We'd like to see if you can come in and identify him?"

Oh. My. Goodness.

"How soon can I come?"

John's eyes asked *what's up.*

The detective responded. "You can come in now if you're available."

Once I hung up and told John who was on the phone, he said he'd take me. I was thankful that I didn't have to go alone.

John put the address in his GPS, so I wouldn't have to direct him back to the city. D.C. had changed so much that it had become unrecognizable over the last fifteen years even if you grew up here.

Even though I was anxious about what would occur at the police station, I managed to ask John a few questions about his life.

"So what's going on with you? I'm sure there is someone in your life even though I don't see a ring. And you mentioned that Christian was your first child." I said emphasizing the word first.

"I have a daughter." He responded sounding hesitant when he continued. "She is from a previous marriage."

At that point, I noticed that the GPS directed him to drive a route that would take longer than the one I knew. I spent the rest of the trip getting John to the precinct because the GPS wasn't doing the best job. I couldn't wait to get all the details of how they found the suspect. This was the beginning of a long journey.

Chapter 14

The heat of the day seeped into the Fifth District police precinct located in the Northeast quadrant of the city. Two factors led to this place being as crowded as Times Square on New Year's Eve: it was the first of the month and hot. I'd say it was 'hotter than July,' but since it was July 1st, it was clear that the calendar and mother nature were in agreement. Police officers shoved handcuffed men and boys through the hallways, some shirtless, some cursing, some high from who knew what. I knew their mamas hadn't seen this in their futures when they were bright-eyed, little boys. I rubbed my stomach and whispered, 'But God.'

I'd told John all of the information that we'd need when we arrived because this dingy, dark and windowless precinct was not what I expected. We didn't see any signs telling us where to go. John spotted a receptionist and directed me that way. As I walked on his heels, we hurried to inquire where we could find Detective Smith. As John spoke to her, I looked around and couldn't help but think how this place reminded me of the set of New York Undercover.

With no words being exchanged, John led me down the hallway, to Detective Smith's office. I was ready to face the man who shot Brian, look him square in the eyes. I knew he wouldn't be able to see me through the one-way glass, but I wished that he could. I wanted him to see that Brian had a wife, a life, and a future until the day he killed him.

As John raised his hand to knock, the door swung open. Detective Smith was on his way out. "Are you Mrs. Jackson?" he asked extending his hand. I shook it and introduced John, although I wasn't sure what to introduce him as, so 'a family friend' was what I landed on.

"Thank you for coming in," he said as he gestured for us to sit in the worn seats in front of his desk. "I know this is hard for you and your family," he said looking between John and me.

He just didn't know how hard, but I was ready to do it. First, I wanted details.

John must've read my mind.

"Detective Smith, can you provide us with any details on how you found this man?"

Although there were manila folders on his desk labeled with Brian's name, he didn't look through them to answer. I wasn't sure how many cases he was responsible for, but I was happy to see that Brian was more than a name on a folder.

"Cameras are everywhere. When the gun went off," he began, looking at me to see if I'd react. I didn't. He continued. "It caused the cameras on the light poles to begin taking pictures. That's the latest technology."

Detective Smith leaned back in his chair before continuing. "The woman he was with wasn't much help. She told us his name, which we got when we ran the fingerprints from a cigarette lighter that he apparently dropped at the scene. She said she didn't know where he was hiding." He added. "His mother was more cooperative than she was."

His mother; that must've been hard.

Finally, I was able to speak. "When will I be able to see the lineup?" Identifying him was important. Justice needed to be served.

For a minute, I forgot that John was there. He was respectfully quiet. But his presence gave me strength.

Detective Smith opened one of the folders and pulled out some pictures. He shook his head. "We don't do lineups. I have five pictures to show you." His eyes showed compassion as he continued. I'll show you the photos, and you let me know if you see the man who shot your husband."

As he carefully laid the pictures on the desk, I looked at him in disbelief. I'd wanted to see that man again. I wanted to study him. He became an important part of my life for all the wrong reasons.

Leaning forward, I studied the pictures; Detective Smith seemed to study me, focusing on my eyes to see if he'd recognize the moment when I saw Brian's murderer. John turned toward me, ready to assist if needed.

The pictures of the men resembled each other. But those eyes, those dark, mean eyes. There was no way I could forget them. The man who shot Brian was in picture number three.

"That's him." I said pointing to the picture.

"Are you sure, Mrs. Jackson?"

I didn't reply at first, I just stared at the picture. I finally answered him. "I'll never forget his face. What's next?"

"I understand. I'll need you to sign a witness statement, and we'll formally charge him with the murder of your husband."

John and I remained in our chairs waiting for more information.

"It wasn't my intent to keep you long today. I'll personally contact you to let you know if we need anything else and the next steps in the process."

This was enough for today. I'd done everything that I could for now.

As we left Detective Smith's office and walked down the hallway, a little boy ran up to me. I recognized him as one of the players on Brian's Boys' Club football teams, but I didn't know his name.

"Miss Lachelle, Miss Lachelle."

"Hi. How are you? What are you doing here?"

Before he could answer, a woman, that I assumed was his mother, walked up to us with tears in her eyes. She told John and me why she was there.

Could this really be true?

Chapter 15

I gave John my address, and he put it in the GPS. The buildings and houses whizzed past as he drove. The sound of my knuckles cracking broke the silence in the car. There were no questions to ask, not much to be said.

Rest was calling my name. But, I knew I couldn't rest until I accomplished two things — telling Tracy and Vanessa what happened at the precinct and giving Tracy a piece of my mind for recommending that I go to the cemetery on the day that she assumed John would be there, too.

After pulling up in front of the house, John paused as if he didn't know if he would be invited in or if I'd say, *'Thank you. I'll see you in another twenty years.'* Weariness reigned supreme, but not rudeness.

"Are you in a rush?" I asked. "If not, you can come in and really meet my line sister. Tracy's car is here so you can catch up with her, too."

"I know what she's doing. Tracy's life is on Facebook."

This confirmed one of my reasons for not being on social media.

After parking behind Tracy's car, John opened my door; still a gentleman. Looming in the air was the smell of burnt hot dogs.

"Someone is getting their Fourth of July grilling started early." John remarked.

Memories of Brian and our annual Fourth of July cook-outs flashed through my mind.

"Smells like it." I responded.

When I opened the door I was surprised to see my girls sitting together in the living room, getting along without adult supervision; Tracy sprawled out on the couch and Vanessa sitting with her legs curled up on the loveseat. "What took y'all so long? I was about to put out an APB." She noticed that our hands were empty and asked, "You didn't bring us anything to eat?"

Bending down to hug Tracy, John commented. "You look the same as you did in high school."

Tracy sat up to receive his hug, then motioned for him to join her.

I re-introduced him to Vanessa who eye-balled him from head to toe.

"So what took so long?" Tracy asked for the second time.

After I got two bottled waters from the fridge and gave one to John, I told them the story: how the detective from the Fifth District station called us.

"Why didn't you call me? I would've met you there." Tracy leaned forward after asking her question.

"Nothing went through my head except getting there as fast as I could. I thought we'd see the suspect live, in person. I thought I'd see him through a one-way window."

"Line sister, you watch too much Law and Order." Vanessa chimed in.

"And for real, Tracy, you don't want to go there with me right now. I have a bone to pick with you later."

Her widened eyes and the forced smile told me she knew exactly what I was referring to.

"May I continue, please?" I asked but looked at Tracy.

She didn't respond but shifted in her seat.

"After I identified the scumbag, I started seeing this thing wrapped up. Knowing that he was still out there walking around, living his life; I couldn't take it."

"You had a long day." Vanessa empathized.

"Soror, you just don't know the extent of it." After joining Vanessa on the loveseat, I recounted the story that still shocked me.

"Miss Lachelle. Miss Lachelle." A voice in the distance called as John and I walked down the hallway.

As I turned, I recognized one of boys from Brian's team pushing his way through the crowded hallway.

"John, wait one second. I know him. I can't remember his name, but he played on one of Brian's football teams."

A woman rushed up behind the boy and grabbed him just as he was about to hug me around my waist.

"Come on, baby, let's go," the woman who I assumed was his mother said, avoiding direct eye contact with me.

"I want to say hi to Miss Lachelle." He said breaking away from her and giving me a hug.

"Hey, baby. What's your name?"

"Jawan. I played running back for Coach Brian. My mommy said that…" Jawan began, but his mother snatched him away from me.

She stepped forward. "Miss Lachelle, I'm sorry about Jawan. They called me down here, and I didn't have anyone to watch him."

A tear fell from her eye, and I asked, "Is there anything I can do? Let's sit down."

Leading her to a few empty seats, John and Jawan followed us. After sitting down, her reluctance to talk was still evident.

"What's wrong? Why are you here?"

"Ms. Lachelle, this is hard. I'm a single mother of two boys. Jawan is my youngest. I've worked two and three jobs to make ends meet."

I wanted to be compassionate, but I was tired, really tired. Compassion won, and I listened.

The words tumbled out of her mouth. "They arrested my son for killing your husband."

Wait. What?

I felt myself pulling away, physically and emotionally. Compassion turned to shock, as I sat back in my chair.

John heard her and spoke. "Maybe it's not the man that you identified. Maybe he is one of the ones who looked like him."

Please God, let that be so.

"Can we see a picture of your son?" John asked.

She pulled out her phone and scrolled to find a photo. I closed my eyes as my heart hammered in the passing seconds. I kept praying that her son was not that man.

Then, I heard her whisper. "Ms. Lachelle."

For a moment, I wanted to keep my eyes closed forever so I wouldn't have to face what God was already telling me was true.

When I opened my eyes, her phone screen was right there. With the photo. It was him. For the second time today, I identified the man who had stolen my husband's life.

What was I supposed to say now? Was I supposed to be sorry? How was I supposed to feel?

John touched my back and whispered. "Maybe we should go. This is a conflict."

"Ms. Lachelle, he's right. But, I want you to know that when I saw my son's face on that TV screen, it broke my heart. I'm a God-fearing woman, and I've raised my sons to be the same. A family member called me and confessed to knowing where

Jeffrey was staying, and it wasn't for the reward money. I called because it was the right thing to do."

Her voice became stronger.

"I called because I didn't want my son to be shot down like a dog in the street."

Why was she telling me all of this? I felt like I was in quicksand. I couldn't move.

She continued. "I just pray that you can find it in your heart to forgive him."

Forgive him.

John spoke up. "Mrs. . . . . . .?"

"My name is Ms. Bryant."

He continued. "Ms. Bryant. I don't think this is the time or place. Lachelle is going through a lot right now, and I'm gonna get her home."

"Yeah, I want to go home." This was enough for one day.

"I understand." Ms. Bryant said. "But, I just hope..."

"Let's go." John took my hand and led me down the hallway. But, there was something I had to do.

I turned around, and Jawan's wide brown eyes were looking at me. He seemed to be about ten years old, but the maturity in his eyes said that he knew more than most his age. I hurried back down the hall.

"God's got this. Be a good boy and listen to your mother, okay?"

"Okay." He sniffled, as if even at his young age, he understood all that was going on, and I could feel that he was torn between his love for his family and his love for Brian.

I blinked myself back to the present and looking at my friends, I could tell that they couldn't believe the police station drama that I recounted.

"It's a good thing that John was there to witness this because I wouldn't have believed what you just told us," Tracy said.

"I need an adult drink after this," Vanessa said, pulling herself up off the loveseat. "Tracy, what do you want me to get you?" Before Tracy could respond, Vanessa added, "Lachelle, I'll get you some Sprite since you can't drink."

I heard crickets.

Out of the corner of my eye, I saw John steal a glance at me. He stood up and grabbed his car keys and his cell phone from the coffee table.

"Yeah, I have an appointment that I almost forgot. So, I'll leave you, ladies, now." He stood up and hurried to the door. I rushed to him. "John. Wait. Let me thank you for everything you did for me today." I walked him to his car.

"You know I got you. Like I told you earlier, you've always been on my mind. I'm not sure what brought us together, but I'd like to call it fate. And it seems that fate left you a gift?"

It was more of a question than a statement. At first, I hesitated. Then I thought about it, he was a pillar of strength for me today. I owed him the truth.

"Yes, I guess you could say that. But, there's more to it, as you very well know."

"Yeah, let's talk soon," he said. He handed me his cell phone. "Would you mind giving me your number?"

I gave him a small smile as I took his phone from him, tapped in my information and handed it back to him. Now, his smile matched mine, and he promised to call me soon to check on me.

I was glad that we parted on a good note. Although today was full of it, I just wanted to get through the next six months as drama free as possible.

Now I had to go back inside and tell Tracy a thing or two about her little surprise.

Once I crossed the doorstep of my house, Tracy handed me my Sprite in a wine glass. She knew my raised eyebrows meant that I was about to broach something serious.

"What prompted you to have me go to the cemetery the day you thought John would probably be there?"

I walked to the couch and sat down; Tracy sat beside me.

Vanessa eased into the kitchen hoping to avoid conflict.

Tracy spoke from her heart. "Lachelle, you know I love you, and I know you. I knew that your hurt wasn't just from Christian's death, but there was never any closure with John. I knew you felt abandoned."

Abandoned. That word shocked me into silence for a moment. Abandonment seemed to be my life's theme. My birth parents abandoned me and gave me up for adoption. I thanked God for my adopted parents. They were older, but stable and loving and I prayed they were resting well in heaven.

Then, my baby was born quiet. My high school love had left me without a thought — or so I thought. And now Brian was gone.

Tracy continued. "I didn't mean any harm. It's just that I knew you would never agree to see John. You're stubborn."

You're right about that.

"Even while mourning Brian, I thought it would help to hear John's side about what happened during high school. We've assumed what happened all these years, but I've followed him on Facebook. Something in my gut told me there was more to the story than John just abandoning you."

I hugged Tracy and spoke from my heart. "You're my sister. I was taken aback, and I knew that it wasn't a coincidence. But, we're good."

"Vanessa we know that you're listening so come on out. I've got something to tell both of you." Tracy yelled in the direction of the kitchen.

On cue, Vanessa strolled into the living room while Tracy flipped through her phone.

"Chicas, how would you like to go to the MGM for a few nights?"

"When today?" I asked.

"Well actually I was trying for this weekend, but it didn't work out. Soooo I was able to pull a few strings and get us a suite there in August before you go back." Tracy said, ending by looking at Vanessa.

Although this was a coup since the resort just opened, I wasn't sure how I felt about going. Would I get sick? Would there be crowds of people?

"I know what you're thinking." Tracy told me. "We won't press you to do more than you feel comfortable doing. If you want to stay in the room with your feet up eating bonbons, that's fine."

Then she got serious. "Let's do something fun. You need some different surroundings."

That was a good point.

"You've convinced me. I'm down to go."

"Block out the second weekend in August, ladies because we are going on a staycation."

Chapter 16

Sleepless nights began after Christian died. Once I married Brian, I slept better because he gave me the best massages. He'd caress my feet and work his way up to my knees, then my thighs. Thoughts of those times swept back to me.

"Roll over so that I can ease your back muscles. That's all you need."

With a prompt shift and smile on my face, I was on my stomach. This was the best part of my day.

Brian's hands went up and down, side to side as if magically putting each part of my body to sleep.

By the time he started easing my temples with rotating circles, I was in dreamland.

"You sleep?" Vanessa asked as she tapped on my bedroom door. Two weeks had passed since we visited Christian.

"Nope. Come on in."

Vanessa wore the cutest and most comfortable pajamas. Tonight she wore a pale blue, satin pants set.

"Aren't you cold? You have this air conditioning pumping."

I wondered why she had on pants.

"I love getting under the covers and wrapping up. Turn the thermostat to what you like. I'm good."

She returned to my room after adjusting the temperature in the hallway.

"I think I'm gonna stay in here with you tonight. Since you have trouble getting to sleep, I thought we'd talk and watch a movie until we both are knocked out."

My arched eyebrows asked *'Really?'*

"You're gonna miss me when I have to leave."

She sat yoga style at the top of the bed, leaning against the headboard.

"Remember when we had to sneak into the dorm during freshman year after going to see the Go-Go bands?" she said while grabbing the remote control from the nightstand.

I had to remind her, "That was you. Always in trouble, trying to pull me in with you."

"But we had fun."

Curling up on the other side of the bed must've felt good to Vanessa. Within twenty minutes of watching *Baby Boy* for the hundredth time, she was knocked out, sleep and snoring. As hard as it was for me to get to sleep, there was no way I'd even get four hours messing with this girl.

"Vanessa. Wake up."

She moaned and rolled over with her back to me.

"Hey," I shoved the back of her left shoulder to get her to wake up.

"What?" she asked snapping her neck back to look at me.

"Go in your room. I'd like to get a few hours of sleep."

"You a trip."

With sarcasm, I asked, as she rolled out of the bed, "Have you seen a doctor about that? It sounds like it's getting worse."

"Bye Felecia," she said before retreating to her bedroom.

I cracked up for the first time in days. It was one twenty in the morning. My twelve-week sonogram was tomorrow and I'd go to work afterward. *Sleep, please be my friend.*

I flipped through the channels. Seth Myers's show went off and Carson Daly's voice filled my room. *Uhmm, maybe I'll go to the DVR.* Wendy Williams, the View or Ellen? Uhm, no exciting guests.

I pushed myself out of the bed and walked across the room to the dresser to get the laptop. I decided to take a look at the MGM Resort to see if there were any special events scheduled for the weekend we were going. The rooms looked spacious, there were a variety of restaurants and Sinbad was the featured entertainment during our staycation weekend. The comedy show might be fun.

I woke up with the laptop still open but it was only three forty in the morning. A little over an hour of sleep. Should I mark that as an accomplishment or a fail? I chuckled, but it wasn't funny; these sleepless nights were back with a vengeance.

Losing sleep because of the ultrasound was not doing me any good. Tracy and I called these sonograms 'peace-of-mind' appointments. But my mind kept going to crazy thoughts: would we hear a heartbeat? Would I pee on the table after drinking all the water? Again, would we hear a heartbeat?

These appointments induced stress. The first trimester down, two more to go. Only. Two. Since my body didn't feel another round of sleep coming, I googled 'the first trimester of pregnancy.'

I saw a picture of a little fetus with the following description: 'The first trimester is the most critical time of your pregnancy. Although the fetus at the end of three months is only about four inches long and weighs less than 1 ounce, all of its functions have begun to form — major organs and nervous system, heartbeat, arms, fingers, legs, toes, hair, and buds for future teeth.'

Rolling over onto my side, I caressed my tummy. Taking slow breaths, willing myself to sleep, I wished Brian was here to hold me, kiss me and love me.

When my eyes opened again, it was only five fifteen. Another sleepless night. The first metro bus would stop at the corner in thirty minutes, and my alarm would ring an hour later.

The alarm buzzed and I slapped at it a few times before shutting it off. The cruelest part was that it felt like I fell asleep only twenty minutes ago.

Although the sheets were warm and called my name, I threw them back and willed my feet to the floor. They obeyed.

As if on cue, Vanessa yelled from downstairs, "Are you up? I'm making breakfast."

Vanessa loved to cook and breakfast was her favorite. A rich, warm cup of coffee might help wake me. I showered, pulled clothes from the closet and dressed. The smell of frying bacon hit my nose as I walked down the stairs, followed by Vanessa's cheerful voice.

"Good morning Sunshine," she greeted me as she took the bacon out of the frying pan. Holding the plate up, with a grin and widened eyes, she invited me to eat.

"I'll put some bacon on toast with an egg."

She grabbed a dishcloth, wiped the pan, grabbed two eggs from the refrigerator and asked, "Scrambled?"

"Yepper." I liked having Vanessa here. She spoiled me, not like Brian did, but in a sister kind of way.

I picked up the tea that she poured but had to steady the cup with my left hand because my hands were shaking. I rushed to put the mug down before Vanessa noticed. I was too late. Her eyes were fixated on my hands.

She didn't say anything, just laid the food down and asked, "Do we have time to eat here or should I wrap it up to go?"

The appointment wasn't until nine o'clock, and it was only seven fifty-five.

"Uhmm, if we leave no later than eight twenty, even in rush hour traffic, we should arrive at eight fifty. We can eat now."

After fixing her B-L-T sandwich, she joined me at the dining room table. "I'll say grace."

We bowed our heads, and when she prayed, I knew why she didn't say anything to me about my nervousness. She took it to God.

"Father God, we come before you to thank you for everything that you have done for us. Even in the midst of what appears to be chaos we know you are our Jehovah-Jireh, our provider. We ask that you rain down peace on us today as we go and check on our little baby. We ask that you guide the hands of the technicians who will oversee the ultrasound. We ask that you send angels to watch over our baby to ensure that every limb grows healthy."

At this point, tears streamed down my face, but I was able to whisper an occasional, "Yes Lord."

Bringing the prayer to a close, Vanessa exclaimed, "Please bless our food that it may provide us with the nourishment that we need to begin our day. We give you all the glory and all the honor. We ask these and all blessings in the name of your Son, Jesus Christ, the Lord. Amen."

"Amen."

I didn't have to tell Vanessa what I needed, she knew. After breathing in and out and wiping my face, I told Vanessa, "Thank you."

Reaching across the table for my hands, she repeated my favorite line from the movie Soul Food. Vivica Fox told Nia Long, during the wedding reception scene, "You my sister gurl and I love you."

After we ate, it was time to leave. Vanessa drove, and we got there in record time.

Thankfully, I was their first appointment. The technician with a bright smile introduced herself as Ms. Lori Woods. She was younger than I anticipated but professional. I loved her neatly kept locs that fell down her back. I introduced Vanessa as my best friend and part of my village.

"It's nice meeting you. The village is important."

We followed her down a short hallway to the room. Once we entered, the brightness of the walls spoke to my spirit, and my heart beat slowed down, a little.

"You can lay here for me." Pulling a chair closer to the examination table, she told Vanessa, "You can sit here if you like."

"Oh, thank you. I appreciate it."

"No problem. I'll leave you now. Oh, let me give you this cloth to put over your tummy until I get back; don't want you getting cool."

She left the room, and I sat on the table, and then rolled my legs over onto it. I wore stretch pants with a cute top, so it was easy to roll them down below my belly.

"This is my first time seeing a sonogram live and in living color." Vanessa gazed at the pictures on the wall as she spoke. Then she turned around. "And I'm glad it's with you." She reached down and hugged me before sitting.

"I'm glad you're here, too."

We heard a light tap on the door.

"Come on in."

"Hello again. So, are you ready to see your baby and hear the heartbeat?" Ms. Lori grabbed the scanner in one hand and the gel in the other which was cold when it hit my stomach. She began rolling the scanner over the gel, spreading it as she went. The room was quiet except for the crackling sound coming from the machine.

We heard nothing. Ms. Lori's voice was optimistic. "I think your baby may be hiding from us. Can you roll over on your side?"

"Either side?" I asked.

"Yes."

I chose the side that had my back to the machine. I didn't want to look at it.

Vanessa eased her hand into mine.

Ms. Lori continued to roll the scanner over my belly.

Nothing. Nada.

Vanessa squeezed my hand.

As she tried to keep a poker face, I saw the concern in Ms. Lori's eyes, but she attempted to reassure me with a tender grin.

Boom. We heard rapid beats from the machine.

"There's our baby." Ms. Lori beamed.

Vanessa let out a sigh of relief.

"Thank you, Jesus." I prayed as tears of joy trickled down my face.

"I'll take a few pictures and then send everything to Dr. Price for her review. But trust me, everything looks good. The receptionist will schedule your follow-up appointment."

Breathe in. Breathe out.

"Thank you, Ms. Lori. You have the best demeanor for this job. I hope I get you when I come back."

Standing near the door, she responded. "I'd love to follow your pregnancy journey. Just verify that I'm in the office on the day of your next sonogram and I'll make sure I see you again."

Reaching my hand out, she stepped forward and enclosed it with both of her hands.

"It was nice meeting you ladies today."

Before she left, she gave me cloths to clean up the gel. Vanessa helped me off the table.

"Now we can go on our staycation with a peace of mind, right?" Her question was more of a statement.

"Staycation, here we come!"

Chapter 17

Within the next three weeks, I went from throwing up every morning to being able to eat whatever I wanted, when I wanted. Foreign smells didn't drive me running to the bathroom, face down in the toilet anymore. For this, I was ecstatic. I was finally through the first trimester of the pregnancy, and I felt a small sense of relief.

Keyword: small.

We anticipated this weekend, and I was ready to go to see if the hotel lived up to the hype.

MGM Casino and Resort was about three miles outside of D.C. But Tracy, rented a limousine to take us.

"We deserve it." she retorted when she showed up at my house to pick us up.

"I'm wit' it." Vanessa happily gave the driver her bags. "Do we have to chip in?"

"Vanessa, I don't do business like that. I'm paying. If I expected anyone else to contribute funds, I would've asked before I rented it. Get in. Let's go." Tracy commanded.

Sliding into the car, I prepared myself for the turn-up. I deserved it.

"Ladies, are you ready?" our driver asked.

"We are more than ready." I responded.

My girls smiled. I was hesitant when Tracy first mentioned the trip. Now that my morning sickness is over, I felt comfortable going out. Besides, rest and relaxation were calling.

I couldn't contain the excitement in my voice. "What happens at the MGM, stays at the MGM. Now let's bust open a can of Sprite." The driver pulled away from the curb.

Vanessa and Tracy broke out in laughter.

As we rode down route 295 south, I couldn't believe the sight in front of us. The MGM was as tall and gorgeous as any Las Vegas resort. The bronze, all glass casino, and resort was a welcomed addition to the area. Other hotels had opened in the area within the last five years. But, the MGM was sure to draw tourists because now East coasters wouldn't have to fly across the country to Vegas to stay at a hallmark MGM resort.

Brian and I had looked forward to coming here to enjoy the restaurants, the shops, and the shows. We'd viewed it online as they built the entertainment complex.

Rounding the curb, we saw the sign pointing to the Tanger Outlets.

"I might have to sneak away and get my shopping on. I read that the resort has complimentary shuttle service to the outlets." Vanessa said, verifying that she knew the location of the outlets in proximity to the hotel.

"Y'all can keep that outlet shopping for yourselves. I'll be at the MCM shop picking me up something cute." Tracy said as she slid her glasses on.

"Okay, so do you teach a finance class? If so, I need to register." Vanessa laughed as she raised her hand for me to give her a high-five. "Tracy you set it out this weekend with the limo and the room. Now you talking about buying from the MCM shop."

We slapped hands while Tracy retorted. "Don't hate the playa."

As we pulled into the circular driveway, the iconic, large gold lions greeted us. The online pictures didn't do the MGM National Harbor justice. It was grand in size and architecture; no resort in the area could compare to its stature. This was what the region anticipated and deserved.

We were greeted with ice cold water as we walked into the lobby. "Yasss, honey, yasss." Tracy exclaimed after taking one sip.

"Okay, so the east coast is trying to rival the west coast. This is grander than the MGM Grand in Vegas." Vanessa noted.

"I'll go and check us in; be right back." Tracy switched her hips toward the reservation desk. Although the lobby was bustling with people, she caught the eyes of a few admirers.

As Vanessa and I sat in the lobby, I noticed the opulence. The orange, green and brown humongous light fixture hanging from the ceiling resembled something out of Star Wars. Everything was so plush, brand new. Yes. We would enjoy this.

As we rode the glass elevator to the nineteenth floor, the people got smaller and smaller, the higher we went.

Tracy used her key to open the door to our home for the weekend. She sashayed into the suite, twirled around and threw her hands out to her sides. "Chicas, what do you think?"

The Capital suite was da bomb. The first thing that took my breath away was the floor to ceiling windows with picturesque views of the Potomac River. In the far distance, I saw planes landing at the Ronald Reagan National Airport. The smell of mahogany caught my nose as I walked toward the work desk. The colors were vibrant, the same as the lobby.

There were two bedrooms. "Lachelle and Vanessa, I'll take this bedroom. I'm sure you all want to catch up on sorority stuff." Tracy kicked off her shoes and buried her toes into the animal skin rug.

After we took our bags to our room, we met up in the living room.

"Thank you for setting up this weekend. I'm glad that we could do this before I had to go back home. Spending time with you guys is important to me and…"

Tracy interrupted Vanessa. "Enough of that mushy stuff. Let's hit these MGM streets."

To make the most of our four days, each of us picked an activity to do that all of us would participate in. Vanessa chose the spa day. The robes were luxurious, and the services were blissful. Even though I didn't get a massage, I met the girls in the manicure/pedicure room dressed as though I did. I chose the comedy show featuring Sinbad.

"It's Saturday night, and I'm warning both of you, I'm putting on my freak 'em dress." Vanessa wrapped her hair up in her signature ponytail.

"You put on your freak 'em dress. I'm putting on my black leather shorts." Tracy told us with a smirk that said *your dress won't touch my shorts.*

Tracy loved sports, so she chose to spend the last night at the sports bar watching a pre-season football game, the Redskins versus the Ravens, the Beltway Battle. The sports bar resembled a meat market; guys eyeing every woman who walked past and the women wearing scandalous attire in an effort to get a free drink and a phone number. The hostess led us to a booth inside the bar although there was outside seating, as well. I was glad because the sun hadn't gone down yet and it was still hot outside.

"What do you guys think about ordering appetizers to share?" I was hungry and wanted to try a few items on the menu.

"Sounds good to me." Vanessa responded as she focused on an attractive guy who I thought might've been a little too young for her.

By halftime, Vanessa had a few too many Margaritas, and her words slurred a bit. "Is that John over there?"

Tracy and I turned in the direction of Vanessa's head nod. John and a nicely shaped woman with medium length hair were standing at the bar laughing, talking and enjoying the game.

Just as I was about to turn around, John leaned his head back to take a sip of his Corona, and he caught me eyeing him.

I wanted to disappear.

I slid up out of our booth.

"I'll be right back; I'm going to the ladies room." Making my way through the crowd, I sensed John moving behind me. Before I could grip the bathroom door, I heard his voice. "Lachelle, wait up."

"Hey? Where did you come from?"

He grinned, and those perfect eyebrows raised up.

"Okay, we saw you, and I didn't want you to see us seeing you." I admitted.

We both laughed.

"How have you been? You look well."

"Thanks. Tracy was finally able to get me to come out for a few days; a staycation."

After a moment of awkward silence, he spoke. "I know that you are not looking for an explanation, but the woman I'm with is my ex-wife. We have a daughter, and when I come to town, we try to do something together so that when we're with her, our friendship is real. It's important to us that Hope knows we get along well, while we're co-parenting."

John was right; he didn't owe me any explanation. But, I was glad he provided one. Why did I feel a sense of relief? My husband died in May, and it was only August — I wasn't looking for another relationship, and certainly not with John.

But when I tried to smile, my lips wouldn't move. I tried to blink away the fuzziness of John's face.

"Lachelle?"

I heard him call my name, but even though he was right in front of me, he sounded miles away. I tried to blink again, but that made my head spin.

"Lachelle?"

John was farther away now. I felt dizzy, and the last thing I heard was John screaming. "Lachelle, what's wrong?"

There was nothing else after that.

Chapter 18

Loud voices woke me up. Tossing my head from side to side, I opened my eyes, but my vision was blurred. While rubbing my eyes, I noticed a strong smell of alcohol. When my vision cleared, I saw rails on a bed. Adrenaline raced through my body as I gripped them and sat up; I remembered falling.

My baby!

"Nurse. Nurse," I screamed. A woman pulled the curtains back and entered. She came over to my bed.

"Is my baby okay?"

"Your baby is okay and so are you." Her soft hand was the opposite of her demeanor. She raised my arm, and when she wrapped the sleeve around me to take my blood pressure, a rush of gratitude swept over me.

"Don't talk. You're at the Southern Maryland Hospital. Your blood pressure increased to dangerous levels, but we were able to stabilize it."

"Have you spoken to my doctor? Are my friends here?"

The commotion from the hallway was too much for me to talk over.

The nurse managed to hear me. "We've spoken to your doctor and are following her instructions."

After shoving a thermometer in my mouth, she looked toward the hallway that was only separated by two thin blue curtains.

"There are three people waiting to get in here to see you."

Tracy, Vanessa, and John.

"Your temperature is normal." Then she turned her attention to another patient calling for a nurse.

"When can I see my friends?"

"You can have one visitor at a time. I'll go out and tell them."

Without saying a word, she turned and raised her right index finger.

Chuckling was a relief. Who would I see first?

The aches and pains of the patients in the immediate area were evident. Just as the sounds got closer to the curtain, John whipped the fabric back.

After throwing his linen blazer on the chair next to the bed, John rushed to me and grabbed my hand. "Hey. They told us that you and the baby are doing okay."

"Yeah, my pregnancy is high risk because of my age and my...history."

His eyes told me how afraid he was before the words flooded out of his mouth. "When you fell, it scared me; my heart almost stopped."

His words surprised me and made me look away.

He squeezed my hand a little. "Over the last month I've been just moving through the day because my mind kept coming back to you."

I turned in his direction, and my eyes became wide with his words, but I said nothing as he grabbed the chair and pulled it closer to the bed. It was much too small for his long torso and legs. He didn't care.

He took another deep breath before he continued. "I'm not trying to scare you or put too much on you, but I have to tell you the truth."

Dude, my husband died just three months ago.

"I won't pressure you for anything except a friendship. If God wants more, we'll know it. But, I want to remain in your life as a friend."

I didn't invite many new people into my life because of my abandonment issues. But, I felt God's spirit ushering in calmness as John spoke. A friendship couldn't hurt.

"Get some rest. I'll be around."

"Okay." I laughed as he struggled with the chair.

As he kissed the back of my hand, we heard Tracy shout. "John, your time is up. Come outta there."

Chapter 19

As the summer heat gave way to end of the season breezes, Dr. Price ordered me on bed rest once I was released from Southern Maryland Hospital. The only thing I was allowed to do was visit a cadre of doctors.

Tracy and John took turns taking me. I tried to schedule most of the appointments on Mondays because Tracy didn't do hair on that day. But on the days when she couldn't take me, John was right there with me; no pressure.

With nothing else to do, my TV stayed on the news channels, CNN and MSNBC. For the first time in my life, I couldn't get enough of this political stuff. I was excited, though. America would have its first female President. I knew there was no way America would vote for an inexperienced, outwardly racist, arrogant throw-back from an era long gone. Who would want to travel back in time after the service of President Obama?

"Emails? Why are you so worried about emails?" I screamed at the commentator trying to over talk Van Jones on CNN. Just then my phone rang.

"Mrs. Jackson, this is Detective Smith from the Fifth District police station. How are you?"

"I'm doing good."

"I hope my news makes your day great."

News?

"The suspect in the murder of your husband is going to take a plea to second-degree murder."

"What's second-degree murder?" I asked as I picked up the remote control to turn down the volume on the TV.

"There was no premeditation on the suspect's part." Detective Smith spoke plainly as though teaching a class. He continued. "We can put him at the scene through eyewitnesses, cameras and his cigarette lighter. He knew there was no need to go to trial."

Then I remembered what his mother told me, that she'd do what she could to ensure he'd tell the truth. I was sure she had gotten through to him.

"With him pleading guilty, how long would his sentence be?"

"Twenty years to life. The prosecution will push for the strongest sentence. The prosecutor assigned to your husband's case is Pamela Wiggins. She will be in contact with you."

I was quiet for a minute, feeling conflicted. Part of me wanted him sentenced to the letter of the law. But then I thought about his mother and his brother. This situation was tearing everybody up. Every second of every day, I had to focus on breathing. I had to focus on staying healthy for my baby. Then I heard that woman's voice. *I hope you can find it in your heart to forgive.*

Could I?

"Mrs. Jackson? Are you there?"

The tissue box fell on the floor as I grabbed for it.

"Yes, I'm here. I guess I'm trying to take all of this in."

"Mrs. Wiggins will send you the date and location of the sentencing. She may talk to you about what's called a victim impact statement."

He piqued my interest even more.

"What's that?" I asked sitting up on the bed.

"Well, it can be either written or oral. But, it's a statement that someone directly connected to the crime makes. It gives the judge an opportunity to hear how the crime has affected the victim or the victim's loved ones."

I'll get a chance to speak for myself, my baby and Brian. Talking to the prosecution was something that I wanted to do now; I was not waiting for them to call me. I wanted to support the state's case. The murderer needed to spend as much time as possible in jail for killing my husband.

"Please email me Mrs. Wiggins' contact information."

"I'll send it to you now."

I thanked Detective Smith, and we hung up. Up next, talking to the prosecution to let them know that I wanted to make a statement on sentencing day. I would do everything that I could to ensure that the murderer was sentenced to as much time as he could get under the letter of the law.

Chapter 20

Fatigue brought on by sleepless nights caused weariness in my bones. The early days of fall had always caused my body to fall into hibernation mode. I guess the darkness brought on by shorter days gave me the winter blues. But, today was the day for the sonogram that should reveal the gender of the baby.

I should have felt happy.

Keyword: should.

Twenty weeks pregnant. My second trimester; I could do this.

As my body lulled itself in and out of sleep, I heard the weatherman mention that today's forecast included rain. A swift change of heart told me that I needed to stay in today. Rescheduling couldn't hurt, just for a day or two.

Grabbing my pillows and tossing back and forth across the bed, various thoughts clouded my mind. The most prominent was that seeing the baby would be like seeing a part of Brian.

Just get up.

Tracy would help me get out of bed. I grabbed my phone which was lying next to me. She'd texted me once, but since the phone was on silent, I didn't hear the notification. Due to the low battery, I plugged it up. Hanging off of the edge of the bed, so that I could talk while the phone was charging, I called her. She answered as if expecting my call.

"Hey. I didn't forget you. I plan to get to your house at ten thirty; a client came in early for a quick wash and blow dry."

Tracy squeezed as many clients into one day as she could. With the mood I was in, she could squeeze a few more in this morning, too. Sitting up on the edge of the bed, gathering strength I told her, "I think I'm gonna reschedule my appointment, I don't feel like it today."

I heard the pitter-patter of light rain against my window, followed by Tracy clearing her throat.

"What happened? You were looking forward to the appointment when we talked yesterday."

Her voice was more calming than I imagined. I admitted, "I'm tired."

"I'll come and help you get dressed. Don't worry about your hair or what you'll put on. I'll take care of all of that when I get there."

Shaking my head, I muttered, "Okay."

Since Tracy was willing to help me, a need to help myself swept over me. I got up and took a shower. Taking a glance in the mirror, it was apparent that Tracy would need to do something with this head. I crawled back in bed and must've drifted to sleep because Tracy's phone call woke me up. It was nine thirty-five.

"I've got some news. But, we can work it out."

Pulling the covers up over my shoulders, I readied myself.

"I have a flat tire."

I didn't comment, and she continued.

"Since Vanessa's gone I think we should call John to take you to this appointment." She knew I'd protest and said, "Hear me out. He's been doing good with following through when we've needed him. I know this appointment is special, and I don't want us to begin canceling appointments. We want to be on top of everything."

Her words sounded like Charlie Brown's teacher.

I look terrible. Wait. Why was I thinking about how I looked?

"Are you there?"

"I'm here."

"Listen to me," she said as I heard cars racing up and down the street as she stood outside by her car. "I know you're scared. But, we want to make sure everything is okay. If Triple-A gets here, I'll join you. But, either way, you'll see me today. Maybe we'll go to dinner."

That would be nice. Even though my test results had been good, I was still scared because I knew I could go to the very end and...

"Let's stay on track with our appointment, okay?"

Through a sniffle, I managed to respond. "You're right."

"Text me John's number and I'll call him to make sure he can do it. Keep your phone charged and near you. Be ready at ten forty either way."

Thank goodness John was in town this week with his D.C. basketball camp.

Tracy called to let me know that John would be there no later than ten forty. "Put a little powder on your face and line your eyes."

I was starting to wonder if this girl really had a flat tire or if this was some type of way to get John and me to spend more time together.

"Tracy, I'm going through with the appointment today, but don't tell me what to do with my face."

"Whateva."

We hung up and I dressed. She kept hair products in the guest bedroom. I called her back and she walked me through which ones to put on my hair so that it stayed down. I grabbed a cute fedora that matched the sweater I wore, walked downstairs and realized I had a little time to spare.

By the time I was ready, it was ten thirty. Lying on the couch I thought about Brian. Lord, I wished he was here. The minute I curled up waiting for John, the phone vibrated alerting me of a text.

John: I'm parked outside the house.

Me: I'll be out in less than five minutes.

Although I didn't anticipate seeing him, it added a sparkle to my day. I'd never tell Tracy, though.

I tossed a few croissants in my bag. Tracy bought them so that I could have something to eat on my way out of the door.

As I pulled the door open, my heart almost fell to the ground. Startled I screamed, "Oh Lord!"

John was standing in the doorway waiting for me. I expected him to stay in the car like he usually did.

"I didn't mean to scare you. It's drizzling and I didn't want you to get wet. I had this huge golf umbrella in my car."

He was right; a small family could fit under it.

When we were together, John was a high school boy, not quite sure of himself and silly. But now...he was a confident, strong, and protective man.

After locking the door, I noticed that the raindrops fell harder. As both of us grabbed the handle of the umbrella, his large hand rested on mine. We glanced at each other for a second. Then we hurried to the car. He opened my door and tucked my raincoat in so that it didn't get caught when he closed it.

I settled in.

"Are we headed to the same office as last time?"

"Same place, same bat channel."

He turned on the car and then the radio. After flipping stations, he settled on WHUR.

Frankie Beverly crooned, "I'm so happy to see you and me back in stride again!"

John turned it up and joined in with Frankie, looking at me, "Back in stride again."

I was glad the song was ending. He was doing the snake.

"John, please stop dancing and drive."

"Okay, okay. But, you have to admit that it was right on time."

I don't have anything to admit.

"I was at the gym when Tracy called. I jumped into the shower and almost did cartwheels to get here."

"You. Are. Crazy."

"That's what they say."

My body relaxed and melted into the leather seats, my legs angled toward him. We were about ten minutes away; we shouldn't be more than five minutes late.

"You know I appreciate you dropping your plans for the morning and helping me. I could've taken Uber."

We came to a stop sign. After pulling off, out of nowhere a car came to a screeching halt. John's arm instinctively shielded me from moving forward.

"What the...?" John screamed.

The driver threw his hands up in the air and mouthed, "I'm sorry."

"Are you alright?"

"I am. I'm good."

"If I was the old John, I'd have gotten out of this car ready to beat him down."

The old John.

"How many Johns are there?"

He turned to glance at me and his raised eyebrows asked, do you really want to know, without saying one word.

"I want to know," I answered him right back.

Leaning into a right turn, he spoke about his past. "I'm not proud of some of the things I've done in my life. Loneliness caused me to run through women when I first joined the NBA. You could say I didn't take their feelings into consideration." As he turned down the radio he continued. "No one wants to be road kill."

His look was pensive and I kept quiet because I didn't want to interrupt his thoughts.

"I'm not using loneliness as an excuse. I'm just glad some Christian players spoke to me and encouraged me to do better."

Before continuing, he stole a look at me.

"The Holy Spirit convicted me and I gave my life to Christ."

He was a Christian. The John I knew in high school didn't go to church or speak about God.

"It sounds like you have a testimony."

"And I share it whenever I can. But, not only do I have a testimony, I have a ministry of working with young men. I don't beat people over the head with my faith, but I don't mind sharing the love that I have for Christ."

It was always good to hear a man talk about the goodness of God. John wasn't a bad boy in school so I shouldn't have been surprised.

We arrived at the doctor's office and there was a small parking lot reserved for the clients. After John squeezed his SUV into a space, we walked into the building and caught the elevator to the third floor.

As we walked down the hallway, my technician, Ms. Lori, walked a couple out of the office door.

"Mr. and Mrs. Battle, I hope you enjoy the rest of your day."

John and I stepped to the side to let the couple pass. As we entered the doctor's office, Ms. Lori greeted us.

"I'm going to step into the ultrasound room to make sure everything is ready for you. Do me a favor and fill these papers out."

She handed the clipboard to me with a pen. John helped me take my raincoat off and hung it up along with his jacket.

Before she headed down the hallway she told us, "I'll be right back for the both of you."

The both of you? Awkward.

I wanted to blurt something out. 'He's just a friend, he's not coming in with me.' But she was gone down the hall.

I was left only with John's smirk. "Well look at it like this. I don't get to see any of your private parts. Don't you just roll down your pants, with only your stomach exposed?

Dis negro here.

"But seriously, you shouldn't go in there alone. Let me be a friend and be here for you now."

He was right. Nothing would be exposed even though it wasn't like he hadn't seen it before, years and years ago.

"Okay. I'll go in and prepare. I'll have Ms. Lori come out to get you when she's ready to begin the sonogram."

"Deal."

I went into the ultrasound room, got ready and while alone, that was when my heart starting beating, faster and faster.

Breathe. Just breathe.

The door squeaked open and I turned my head toward it. The fear in my eyes must've screamed out to John because he hurried over, sitting in the chair next to the table. He didn't say anything, but he held my hand.

"Are you okay, Mrs. Jackson?"

Am I okay? My stomach was doing flips and it was not the baby.

"I'm fine. I'm ready."

"Before we get started, I need to ask, do you want to know the gender or do you want to be surprised?"

I had thought about it and I wanted to know. I was stressed enough. I didn't want that question to weigh heavy on my mind.

"I want to know today."

"Then let's get started. And we're doing the three-dimensional ultrasound. You requested that one, right?"

They said these new sonograms allowed you to really see your baby. When I checked the box, it wasn't with optimism. I thought back to Christian and wished they had this type of technology around back then. I would've seen him, at least once.

Ms. Lori grabbed the gel and squeezed it onto my tummy. With the sensor, she spread it across the baby. The only sound in the room was the gurgling from the machine.

Since I was further along in the pregnancy, hearing the heartbeat wasn't a problem this time; it was strong.

My baby moved its legs, arms and appeared to turn to the camera and wave.

"Hello to you, too, baby." I couldn't help myself. I chuckled as a tear of joy streamed down my face.

In silence, John wiped it away.

"I'm not sure if the baby will position itself so that we can see the gender."

Ms. Lori moved the sensor and moved the sensor. I turned on my right side and my left.

Just when Ms. Lori was about to put the sensor away, she exclaimed, "Mrs. Jackson, look, right here. I'm glad that we didn't give up because we know what you're having."

Yes!

Chapter 21

Looking out of my bedroom window, I saw God in the crimson, mustard and plum colored leaves. Although it was dark, the moon's glare reflected off of fall's colors. Every day seemed to bring something new; days of darkness and days of light. The dark days brought thoughts of death, memories of past pain. The lighter days gave me joy, especially when kicks of life moved inside my tummy. I went from being able to move around easily, to holding onto items to ensure that I didn't take a tumble. Swollen legs hid my ankles. Dr. Price took me off of bed rest.

As I laid there, I heard the faint sound of a song coming from the spare bedroom, Vanessa's playlist.

I told the storm to pass, storm you can't last. Go away, I command you to move today.

I sang this song, 'I Told the Storm', back in the day with the choir.

Death can't shake me, job can't make me, bills can't break me, disease can't take me, you can't drown me while God surrounds me, That's what I told the storm.

The tears fell and fell, saturating my pillow. Tomorrow morning was sentencing. I thought it would be appropriate to pray the same words that Christ prayed in the Garden of Gethsemane the night before His trial. Before falling asleep, I prayed the Lord's Prayer. I couldn't kneel down beside the bed as I normally did, so I sat on the edge and clasped my hands together and began to talk to God.

"Our Father which are in heaven, hallowed by Thy name. Thy kingdom come, Thy will be done on earth, as it is in heaven. Give us this day our daily bread. And forgive us our debts, as we forgive our debtors…And forgive our debts, as we forgive our debtors. Forgive us…"

Gripping the sheets, while rocking back and forth, I whispered. "Heavenly Father I know what I must do; just like Jesus knew that He had to do while praying in the Garden of Gethsemane. He didn't want to, and I don't want to, but give me a listening ear to hear your voice."

~~~~~~~~~~~~~~~~~~~~~~~~~

John, Tracy, Vanessa and I arrived at the courthouse thirty minutes before the trail began. Vanessa flew in a few days ago and John was adamant that he attend. "I was there when they called you to identify him. I want to see this all the way through." He wasn't taking no for an answer and I agreed with him. I grew accustomed to him by my side.

The building was active with people. As we got closer to courtroom number thirty-three, I saw people milling around. I recognized some of them as local TV reporters. Instead of waiting in the hallway we entered and sat in the second row on the prosecutor's side. I noticed Ms. Bryant seated on the defendant's side surrounded by family or friends. Their looks were intense as they listened to the defense lawyer.

When Ms. Bryant glanced my way, our eyes met for a second.

Just before it appeared that the sentencing would begin, I saw Keisha out of the corner of my eye. I waved her over where we were; she settled into a seat directly behind me.

I stretched my hand over my shoulder and greeted her. "I'm so happy to see you."

"You know I was coming." She told me, as she glanced over at the people sitting on the other side. "I wanted to see this bama."

I patted her hand which was resting on my shoulder. I turned around and noticed that the courtroom didn't look anything like the ones on TV. It looked like it seated one hundred people. What struck me most was the orange and brown décor; it resembled the colors of a warm living room. I envisioned hardwood floors and a large wooden area surrounding the judge; but not here. Interior decorators carefully planned the matching earth tones. I wondered why.

The door in the front of the courtroom opened; two marshals brought Jeffrey Bryant, handcuffed, into the courtroom; wearing black pants, a white shirt, a black tie and what appeared to be a pair of personality glasses.

Umph.

He looked around to see who was there, when his eyes met his mother's, she mouthed to him. "Be strong."

When he saw us, he quickly turned his eyes and sat down next to his lawyer. I'm sure Keisha's gaze identified us as Brian's family.

The courtroom clerk's voice grabbed my attention. "All rise."

We all did. Once the judge rushed through the door and took his seat, we sat, as well.

Suddenly the courtroom clerk's voice permeated the room again. "Calling the case of the District of Columbia v. Jeffrey Bryant. Mr. Bryant, are you here?"

Answering in his stead, his attorney responded, "He is here."

I wonder if everyone in the courtroom could hear my heart pumping against my chest.

The judge went through a litany of questions for the murderer and read the facts of the case. When asked if the facts were true, Jeffrey bowed his head then slightly raised it, responding, almost in a whisper. "Yes."

Where were the tears?

Looking through some papers the judge peered over his glasses. "Thank you, Mr. Bryant. Does the prosecution have anything to say?"

The prosecuting attorney rose from her seat. "Judge Hamilton, I'd like to call Mrs. Lachelle Jackson to the stand to present her victim impact statement."

John, Vanessa and Tracy all tried to assist me as I stood. I was determined to get up without any assistance and walk to that stand in the same manner.

I mouthed to them, "I'm okay." They stepped into the aisle to let me pass.

As I walked up to the stand I heard whispers in the courtroom, but felt the tugging of the Holy Spirit.

And forgive us our debts…

Hush Holy Spirit.

As we also have forgiven our debtors.

I didn't want to. But, I felt the power of the Holy Spirit bubbling beneath the surface. It spoke to me.

"Your Honor, I am Brian Jackson's widow. I've lost a big part of my life. My husband was a pillar of this community. He mentored boys and worked to ensure that you would never see them standing before you."

The murderer's eyes were big as saucers and his mouth gaped open. He didn't know that I was going to say. Neither did I.

I cleared my throat and continued. "I've spoken with my husband's assistant coaches and I learned that the defendant was involved in his much younger brother's life in a positive way, before this tragedy. I asked the coaches if the defendant knew my husband and they said no. The football field was typically crowded with kids and parents before and after the game. They never met face to face."

As I began to end my statement I glanced at his mother. Her eyes were closed with her hands clasped in a praying position. I read her lips as she repeated the same prayer. "Thank you, Lord."

"The one thing that I would ask you to consider is the defendant's positive influence on his brother, before this tragedy. I'd ask that you consider Jawan, and his mother, as you sentence him."

The judge removed his glasses. "Thank you, Mrs. Jackson. I'm sure that wasn't easy. The court appreciates your candor. You may step down."

As I walked, my eyes focused on my seat. There was no urge to look at anything besides my seat and my support. I wanted to beg the judge to lock him up forever. But, the Holy Spirit guided my spiritual fortitude and I was obedient.

Once I sat down, the judge continued. "I have letters from the defendant's mother and her pastor. They both reiterated that Mr. Bryant was a good student through school but lost his way with drugs. They gave the same backstory provided by

Mrs. Jackson. Is there anything that you would like to say to the court, Mr. Bryant?"

He looked behind him and found his mother. Dabbing her cheeks with a tissue she mouthed the answer to the question that his eyes asked. "Say, I'm sorry."

He obeyed his mother. "Your Honor, what I did was an accident. And I'm sorry."

That's when his tears began to flow.

"It's time for the sentencing." The judge's stern baritone voice announced with decisiveness. "After taking everyone's statements into account, I hereby sentence Jeffrey Bryant to twenty-five years to thirty years in prison."

I released a long sigh. The murderer was twenty-seven years old; he could be released from prison at the age of fifty-two. He should be relieved that he would still have some of his life to live.

That was when I began to look at him. I watched as the marshals handcuffed him. He wasn't any taller than five foot eight. Brian would've beat him down in a fair one-on-one fight. I kept my eyes on him as he went through the door. Just before it closed, he turned, looked at me and said, loud enough for everyone to hear him. "Thank you."

I just sat there. *Is it over?* I knew the answer to that, and it was, no. I'd live with this for the rest of my life. But this part of the story was over, and that offered some relief.

John rose to talk to one of the lawyers, while Tracy held my hand. "You ready, honey?" She asked.

"I am."

Helping me rise and keeping me steady on my feet, Tracy put my coat around me.

Chapter 22

It was the Saturday after Thanksgiving, a sunny but blustery autumn day. The world was darker now because the November eighth Presidential election put an apparent racist, sexual predator and outright fool in the White House. No one knew what to expect. What advances would he roll back that would have long-term ramifications?

Thanksgiving was a season of counting our blessings, and I thanked God for so much. Although I missed Brian, every day, I was thankful for my girls who decided that they wanted to throw me a baby shower. I didn't want one, but I told them that if I had to have one, it couldn't be a surprise. I needed to know the date.

Tracy and Vanessa agreed because of my condition. They planned it for the Saturday after Thanksgiving, and that was all I knew; the rest was a surprise.

My other condition was that the baby's gender wouldn't be made public. Again, they agreed.

Tracy and Vanessa told me to be ready promptly at two o'clock, when a driver would pick me up and take me to the celebration. I changed clothes at least three times.

The sound of the hawk blowing outside told me to dress in layers. I'd been getting warm lately, so I thought a cute, sleeveless, collared blouse under a burnt orange and brown sweater would be good. Leggings and Uggs would ensure comfort. I topped the look off with a brown cape, trimmed in faux fur. I was cute.

When Tracy told me that a driver would pick me up, I assumed a limousine driver.

Keyword: assumed.

I was standing in front of the window waiting when John pulled up in front of the house, jumped out of the car, and grabbing his hat so that it wouldn't get carried away by the wind. My eyebrows rose in surprise.

Before he could ring the doorbell, I gripped the doorknob and attempted to slowly open the door, but the wind forced the door against the wall and carried John into the house.

"Shawty, this wind is disrespectful."

I grabbed the thickest shawl wrap that I had while staring at him. He sounded as though I knew he was coming to get me.

"Why are you looking at me like that?" he asked with a frown. "Didn't they tell you I was picking you up?"

"I didn't realize you were coming to the shower."

"Lachelle, I ain't trying to go to no shower. I told Tracy to let me know how I could assist and she asked me to pick you up and drop you off. That's it. That's all."

I knew some of Brian's family would be there to celebrate and I didn't want any drama; even though John and I were just friends.

"I'm not trying to be mean, but..."

"No explanation is necessary. I'm just here to help. I don't want you to feel as though you have to explain who I am to those who don't know me, yet."

Keyword: yet.

"John, you really need to stop."

"I'm just teasing. Are you ready? I don't want Tracy and Vanessa beating me down for getting you there late."

After he helped me with my cape, we walked to the car. My girls didn't give me much information so I thought I'd see what I could get from John.

"Where are we going?"

He looked at me as though I was crazy.

"To your baby shower. Duhhh!"

"I mean where, as in location, fool?"

"You'll see when we get there. Don't ask many more questions. I'm sworn to secrecy."

John skipped the subject and told me about his foundation and the work that he was doing in the community with both boys and girls.

I was impressed.

"I created a foundation to serve the communities in the cities where I've played. Every summer we run basketball camps in the underserved sections of the cities, boys and girls can enroll."

Turning the corner, he continued. "In two of the cities that I've played in, we're emulating Steve Harvey's mentoring program for young boys where we bring in some ballplayers to talk about life skills and of course, shoot some hoops.

Just as I imagined John with the boys and the girls, I noticed we were a few blocks from my church.

"I know where we're going."

"Well, you should. But, you ain't heard it from me."

Laughter filled the car.

I motioned to direct John to the entrance of our church hall. I was relieved that they knew I'd be comfortable at church. They didn't spend too much money and I really loved that.

John parked and ran to my side to open the door. Just as I swerved my legs to get out of the car I saw Keisha sitting in hers across the street from the church putting on make-up; our eyes met. Her mouth dropped when she saw John open the door for me. I wasn't sure if I had enough time to tell John to get back in the car and just drive away.

Keisha got out of the car and must've forgot something because she turned on her heels and headed back to her car. Thank you, Lord.

"John, act like an Uber driver and just leave before Brian's sister gets over here. That's her." I said tilting my head to the side.

"Let me say bye to the baby. You know it'll miss me." John replied with a sly grin.

I wanted to whack him but mouthed through clenched teeth. "Get out of here."

He laughed. "No problem. I'll hit you up to see if y'all need help taking…"

I barely heard the ending of what John said as I walked into the all familiar church foyer. Keisha came in behind me, huffing and puffing. Did she run after me?

"Oh hey, Keisha."

"I should 'hey' you. Who was that? My brother died six months ago and you already got a new man?"

"First of all, don't start no mess today. And second of all, that was my ride here. If he was my man, he would've come inside. I don't have anything to hide from you."

The focal point of the grandiose church foyer was a body length gold trimmed mirror. Keisha took a minute to look me up and down while I glanced in it lying my hair down.

My friends must've realized that I was in the foyer. Hushed voices replaced the conversations I heard coming from the multi-purpose room. Our sanctuary was gorgeous, but the multi-purpose room was always the warmest place in the building to me. I couldn't wait to see how Tracy and Vanessa decorated it.

"I'm going in now." I told Keisha.

"I'll let you walk in by yourself. I know you don't want me ruining your moment."

The look of disdain on her face hurt me. But, I wasn't going to focus on that. It was time for me to enjoy what my girls had planned for me.

Breathe. Just breathe and enter.

Anticipation grew as I pulled the large, wooden double doors.

"Surprise!"

I looked over a sea of family, friends, sorors, colleagues, and schoolmates. And Brian's family was there in full force. I was surprised to see males there too. It was a coed baby shower.

After I scanned the faces, I noticed the beauty of the room. Lovely pink and blue pintuck tablecloths sat under centerpieces filled with cute African-American babies, boys and girls. Sashes of the same color wrapped around the chairs for guests and balloons filled the air. The fireplace was lit which added to the warmth of the room. There was a selfie section with props and pink and blue cupcakes.

Tracy and Vanessa hugged me. Vanessa whispered as she smiled. "Just act like it was a surprise."

They led me to a regal chair, fit for a queen in the center of the room.

I couldn't help but to think about Brian and how happy and proud he'd be at this moment.

My guests and I took selfies, filling the room with love and laughter. Vanessa led the games. The first one we played was to see who could guess the width of my tummy using toilet paper, some of the ladies almost used an entire roll. Wrong. But, Sister Maxine's guess won the prize.

"Vanessa, please give her a big gift bag because she was nice in her guess and still won."

She moseyed up to the front to get her gift with her cell phone in her hand, she snapped a picture with Vanessa, "You don't mind, do you, baby? I told some of my co-workers I'd see you today."

"Of course I don't. Let's give them duck lips."

And duck lips they did.

Tracy and a few friends from church served non-alcoholic, signature drinks, Rubber Ducky punch, in champagne flutes. The buffet line flowed well, no long lines at any one time. We dined on the best African-American cuisine, fried chicken, string beans and macaroni and cheese.

And the cake. It was the most gorgeous, cutest and tastiest cake I had ever tasted.

"Do we have to cut the little brown babies on the sides?" Those ponytails on her look so real, and those Jordan's on his feet. Who made this cake?"

Tracy laughed. "I'll try not to cut too much of the babies. Details later." After we'd eaten, we sat in a circle, and First Lady Kendra stood. "This is the time when we're going to give you advice; our pearls of wisdom. I want you to remember that you have a village who will always be there to help you."

Attending baby showers hadn't been one of my favorite things to do in the past, but when I attended them, this time of the shower was always my favorite.

Lady Kendra encouraged others to come up. "Now, I know I'm not the only one who has words of wisdom. Who's next?"

People picked up their champagne flutes, looked at their phones and did other things to avoid speaking. I heard the squeaking of a chair and saw Janis, my co-worker, strutting up to the front.

She tapped the microphone before speaking. "There was no way I could let today pass without telling you how I love you, or I'll say how much *we* love you. Will everyone here from Loving Our Babies please stand."

Six of my co-workers stood at their places.

"Not only are you our supervisor but our friend. Remember to love yourself as much as you love everyone in your life and that baby will grow to be happy, filled with joy."

With my arms outstretched I reached up, and she walked over to my chair and reached down to hug me.

"Thank you for that reminder. You know it's hard sometimes."

"Just remember I'm here and can't wait to babysit."

Brian's Aunt Louise from Philadelphia had a full Pentecostal moment when she stepped to the microphone.

Without blinking an eye, she began. "This is the day that the Lord has made and we will rejoice and be glad in it. Will everyone from the Jackson side of the family stand."

At least ten people did as Aunt Louise directed. From the time that I spent with her while Brian was alive, I knew that she craved attention. She got it today.

"Lachelle, we are Brian's blood family. And my nephew loved him some you. Although he is not here in the body, we are. We'll be here to help you raise that baby in the Lord. Stay focused on Proverbs twenty-two and six which says, 'train up a child in the way he should go and he will not depart from it.'"

Then I noticed her feet moving, faster and faster and she broke out into a shout. Her husband, Uncle Cleveland, got up and assisted her back to her seat.

Tracy and Vanessa stepped to the forefront together to share their wisdom with me, and already I had tears in my eyes because their love permeated my heart.

But before they could speak, Keisha stood and tapped her spoon against her flute. One of Brian's cousins encouraged her to sit down, but she didn't. "No, I'm gonna get this off my chest."

Tracy gave me a look. *I'm giving her the hook.*

With my eyes, I signaled. *Let her talk.*

Tracy gave Keisha the microphone and the look that everyone could interpret. *Don't play with me.*

Keisha rolled her eyes. "Word on the curb is that I don't like my sister-in-law. I want to set the record straight."

Sister-in-law. Uhm, first time I've ever heard her call me that.

"My brother was so much to me; brother, father figure and my best friend. I want to keep it real wit' y'all. I felt that Lachelle took my brother away from me. But, that's all squashed." Looking at me directly, she continued. "I ain't got nothing against you. I wish you happiness and I know that you and the baby will be fine. Shoot, I hope you let me babysit."

Babysit? She was going a bit too far. That probably wouldn't happen until my baby could talk, walk and everything else.

Appreciating her openness, I got up to hug her but felt woozy. I stumbled as I walked toward her. Tracy and Vanessa's eyes widened. Before everything faded to black I felt arms around my waist and heard Vanessa scream. "Lachelle."

Chapter 23

After fainting at the baby shower, Dr. Price ordered me to stay home on bed rest for a week. My blood pressure was higher than she would've liked, but not high enough to admit me into the hospital.

I kept Brian's crumpled paper with baby names under the pillow on his side of the bed; the one with his cologne scent. I studied the paper. Brian was my angel and this note was proof that God allowed him to speak to me from heaven.

Tracy stayed with me while I was on bedrest but she worked late this evening. I laid on the bed, flipping channels, landing on 'This Christmas', the movie with Idris Elba and Chris Brown. As I laid the note on my chest, right above my heart, my text alert rang. It was probably Tracy telling me that she was on her way here.

I leaned up and pulled the phone from my nightstand almost knocking over the bottled water.

I was surprised but I shouldn't have been. The text was from John, asking me how I was doing.

Me: I'm doing well. I go back to the doctor in two days for a follow-up.

Him: I can't bust you outta that joint yet?

Me: Not yet. I'll keep you posted.

Him: Do that. Get some rest.

Me: Thank-you

Would I let him know when I was released from bed rest? He expressed that he always thought about me over the years. But he promised to be a friend and he had kept his promise. Was it wrong for me to want to hang out with him?

Brian had been gone six months and part of me felt that it was too soon to go out. I mean I didn't go online or anything. I didn't go on social media finding anyone. He was at the cemetary. The cemetary...Brian led me there. Was that a sign?

That week, Dr. Price gave me approval to get back on my feet. "Take things slow. Don't rush into your normal routine."

"I won't. I promise you. These fainting spells have scared everything out of me."

While driving home, Tracy's message was, "I've got my eye on you." I loved her for that.

"Let me run this past you." I thought that it might be a good time to sneak in the fact that I was considering going out with John. And I did.

"Chica, go out and enjoy yourself. You wouldn't be doing anything wrong. Okay? Get that out of your head."

And as in Tracy style, she followed up with a funny. "I can't tell you to go get your groove back, because you never really had one. But have fun."

"Whateva." We couldn't contain our laughter.

After letting John know that I could hang out, but nothing strenuous, he responded. "Don't worry, I gotchu. We're not going parasailing."

"I know that. I just needed to say it."

"Seriously, I wouldn't put you in harm's way. We can stay in if you prefer."

I didn't feel comfortable having John in my house, Brian's house, like that yet. It felt like cheating.

"I need out of the house."

Saturday arrived and I was ready to enjoy a night out.

Tracy did my hair and helped me pick out a cute maternity outfit; plum colored stretch jeans and a navy blue blouse that flowed as I moved. My cute low heel boots still fit me, although my ankles were a bit swollen. She had her own date so she left the house a little before me.

It was six-fifty; dark because the days were shorter. John was supposed to arrive at seven o'clock. I peeped out of the living room blinds. John was outside leaning against the passenger door of his midnight black on black Cadillac Escalade.

The light from his cell phone illuminated his caramel brown face outlined by his dark mustache and goatee. His olive green suede jacket hung nicely on his lean six foot seven frame.

I'd seen John over the past few months but tonight I was really seeing John. Whew! This man was fine.

I was sure that he didn't want to scare me by coming to the door like he did last time. I called him so he'd know I was coming out.

As I walked down the stairs, his grin told me we were gonna have a nice evening.

Just hanging out.

"What's up, Miss Lachelle?" He opened the car door and helped me up into the SUV.

I felt like a kid on Christmas morning. "Where are we going?"

Pulling off he told me his plans. "I thought you might like riding around for a while looking at the Christmas lights."

My mouth dropped open.

"Close your mouth. You didn't think I'd remember that you loved riding around looking at the Christmas decorations when you were younger?"

My father, mother and I would ride around town when I was a little girl looking at the lights on the houses and the decorations of the department stores downtown.

"I haven't done this in the longest time."

At that point, snow fell, painting a soft white blanket on the ground. The alluring silver and gold trimmed decorations adorned the stores in Georgetown. I even heard the Salvation Army Santa Claus sounding the call for donations and his hearty, "Ho, Ho, Ho."

The houses were just as beautiful. Lighted reindeer and huge Santas filled the yards.

Turning my head away from the joy that felt like it was seeping through the window, I faced John. I didn't say one word, but I gave him a look to let him know that I cherished this surprise.

"Oh, the lady is impressed."

"I am."

"Ready to eat?"

My attention had been so focused on the beauty of the city lights and the snow that I didn't think about my empty stomach.

"Absolutely. What did you have in mind?"

"Is seafood good for you?"

"Yes, yes and yes."

We hit route fifty east to head to Bowie, MD. Jerry's Seafood was a metropolitan favorite. The snow must've kept people away because we only waited ten minutes for our table, a little before eight thirty.

As the hostess walked us to our table, John followed me, touching the small, intimate part of my back, right above my butt. It threw me for a second, but I didn't turn around nor did

I swat his hand away. Although it felt a little uncomfortable, he was just being a gentleman.

Fidgeting with my napkin, I inspected the menu.

"Are you okay?"

My nervousness was obvious. I hadn't been on a date with anyone other than Brian in fourteen years.

Just hanging out.

I threw down my napkin. "I'm fine."

We enjoyed calamari as an appetizer. Both of us ordered their signature crab bomb for our meal. Lump crab meat filled the bomb, very little mayonnaise to hold it together with absolutely no filler; exquisite.

"We literally stuffed our faces."

He was right. I decided to ask a question that I'd been wondering about, not sure why, but the thought had crossed my mind. "Do you consider D.C. home?"

He wiped his mouth and seemed to contemplate the answer. "D.C. will always be my home. But, I have roots in the other cities where I've played; Dallas, Minnesota, and Houston. Once I left for college, I never really moved back here to live."

After picking up a fork full of broccoli, and chewing it much longer than I would've, he continued. "My mother planned my life for me."

That surprised me. John's mom was very controlling. She pushed him to play basketball; that was obvious when we were young. But, I didn't realize that he recognized just how controlling she was.

"But don't get me wrong, I wanted to play ball and it's afforded me a great life."

That was one thing that impressed me with this evening, John made a nice salary playing for the NBA but he kept it low key, focusing on me and what I'd like. He could've done anything tonight, from renting out a restaurant to sailing down the Potomac River on a yacht.

"To answer your question, I plan to settle down here in the D.C. metro area. My daughter's here. I owe her that."

My chest deflated with a sigh of relief. Why?

After John paid the bill his attention returned to me. "Miss Lachelle, are you ready?" He leaned onto the table and looked at me, I mean really looked at me. I leaned forward, too.

"I feel tight as a tick."

We both laughed.

"I'm glad that you enjoyed dinner."

"I enjoyed the evening. Thank you for getting me out of the house and into these streets."

He stood up and reached for my hand. I took it and we walked out of the restaurant to the car.

By the time we arrived at my house, I had fallen asleep. John woke me up, smoothing my hair away from my face.

How did John know that physical touch was one of my love languages? I smiled at him. "Well, I'll get on in this house. The baby and I need to get some rest."

"Okay. And I hope we can do this again. Soon."

He got out and jogged around to my side of the car. After he opened the door, we walked up to my door.

"I'm glad that you enjoyed your evening." He took my hands in his. "You know we can call this 'the remix'."

Nooooo. Don't kiss me.

His lips kissed my forehead. Then he tilted my head upward.

Nooooo.

John pecked me on the lips and kissed my nose. "I'll call you when I get home."

I nodded.

Then he jogged down the sidewalk and hopped in his SUV. He watched me open the door and go inside. I waved goodbye.

The remix.

Chapter 24

A few weeks passed and I felt like a stack of buttermilk pancakes with butter dripping off the sides; just good.

"Light the fireplace." Vanessa had flown back into town for Christmas and because I was thirty-four weeks pregnant. One thing Vanessa loved about the East Coast was the winter. We couldn't get her out of those Uggs.

The smell of the live Christmas tree that we decorated a week before permeated the living room.

After Tracy lit the fireplace, we sat on the floor to wrap a few dozen Christmas gifts; John's foundation would deliver them to foster homes and shelters on Christmas Eve. In anticipation of delivering a few gifts ourselves, Vanessa purchased three very ugly sweaters which were lying on the couch.

"I'm not wearing that sweater," Tracy told us. "Don't they have some sexy ugly sweaters?"

"That would defeat the purpose," Vanessa responded with a smirk.

Leaning against the couch to support my back, I rubbed my right temple. I'd had a nagging headache for a few days that didn't want to go away.

"I've seen you do that a few times today." Tracy's eyes stayed on me waiting for a response.

"It seems like a headache that wants to stay around."

"Let's call the doctor." Tracy got up and pulled my purse off of the dining room table. "I'm trippn' that you didn't say anything."

Pulling the medical card out, I complied with her request and called. They told us to come into the office.

Vanessa helped me up off of the floor, "Better safe than sorry, right?"

I lifted my arm so that she could help me up. She grabbed my boots while Tracy grabbed my coat. I still didn't feel like anything was wrong, just this slight headache. But, I agreed with them, better to waste a few hours at urgent care than regret not going.

We piled into the car after putting out the fireplace and locking everything up.

Our ride was short and I focused on the beauty of the city. There was nothing like this time of the year.

We arrived and I checked in, Vanessa walked with me while Tracy parked the car.

It was Christmas Eve's Eve, so not many people were there. Once I explained everything to the advice nurse, they were expeditious in their movement. They took my vitals and blood.

Tracy and Vanessa were with me when they completed the sonogram. When we heard the baby's heart all three of us let out an audible sigh of relief.

Within ten minutes the doctor on call came in to tell me that I would be admitted to the hospital because my pressure was too high and that I had developed preeclampsia.

"Your baby is fine. But, we want to monitor you over the next day or two. If your pressure doesn't come down, we'll consider inducing labor."

Due to the apparent severity of my case, they called an ambulance to take me to the hospital. The urgent care personnel assisted by placing me on the cot, then rolling me out to the ambulance. Tracy and Vanessa scurried out with us one on each side of me. Vanessa rode in the ambulance while Tracy followed us in the car. They stayed with me that night.

When they were sound asleep, my nurse introduced herself. "I'm Nurse ReAnn and I'll take care of you while you are here." Her smile was nice and her demeanor warm. "I'm sure that the last place you wanted to be on Christmas Eve was here in the hospital, but we'll take great care of you and your little one."

I nodded my affirmation and smiled. I was tired. The beeping from the monitors lulled me to sleep.

~~~~~~~~~~~~~~~~~~~~~~~~~~~~~~~

The Christmas Eve sun made its way through the blinds and woke all three of us up. I convinced them to go home and get my bag for me.

"I think one of us should stay with you."

"I'm fine. I really want you both to help John deliver some of those toys."

They both gave me a look that asked, 'What have you been smoking?'

"No really. I looked forward to this and I want y'all to represent me."

Tracy put her hand on her hip.

With a pout, I pleaded. "Please, do that for me; pack some of my things from the house and at least make one delivery to the kids."

They looked at each other.

"Okay, and once we come back, we are not leaving this hospital without you," Vanessa was the first to respond.

"Deal?" I said to Tracy with my pinky finger held high for her to grasp like we did when we were kids. Her grip was her confirmation.

"Do me one favor and text John first. I want him to know what's going on."

Tracy texted him and within two minutes her phone rang. She answered. "Hey."

Tracy turned the speaker on so that we all could hear.

John sounded upset. "What happened? Is she okay?"

Tracy continued. "She's fine but her blood pressure is higher than they would like so they want to monitor her.

"Where is she? Can she talk?"

"She can talk. Hold on."

I reached for the phone. "Hey, John."

"What in the world happended?"

"I had a headache that wouldn't go away late last night."

He almost didn't allow me to complete my sentence before asking his question. "Why didn't you call me then?"

"We didn't call you because it was late and we fell asleep."

Silence pierced through the phone for a second before he continued. "I think I should leave the toy deliveries to volunteers and come see you."

I maintained a strong voice so he'd know that I was fine. "No. This is major for the foundation. The kids want to see you. Don't disappoint them. You know the doctors just want to be careful."

"Ugh. You're right. They've pumped these kids up."

"You know I'm right. Take care of the deliveries and I'll see you later." He didn't respond. I continued. "I'm good."

"Okay. I'll see you soon, very soon."

"See you later." I ended the call and handed Tracy her phone.

Vanessa chimed in while putting on her coat. "That brother cares about you."

"He does, but what is it that they say, it's complicated."

After kissing me goodbye, they left.

About an hour later, Nurse ReAnn came in with breakfast. I ate some but wasn't really hungry.

"Ms. Lachelle, if you don't want that then I can get you something else. Toast? Tea?"

My eyes were heavy and I didn't understand why because I had gotten a good night's rest. Then I tried to smile at Nurse ReAnn but I couldn't even move my lips, they almost felt paralyzed.

From the TV that hung in the corner of the room, I heard Steve Harvey say, "And the number one answer is," but with the way my lids were lowered, I couldn't even see what rolled over on the board.

Finally, I allowed my eyes to completely close, and then a second later, frantic shouts came from Nurse ReAnn. "Code Blue, Code Blue!"

Over her voice, there were beeps and alarms, and then other voices before there were louder beeps and alarms.

Something was wrong. That was my second to last thought. My final thought: *Jesus, Jesus, Jesus!*

Chapter 25

A cool, light breeze woke me up. The smell of salt raced up my nose. My fingertips buried themselves in, what felt like, soft sand. I was in heaven, I was sure of it.

If I could have mustered the courage to move, I would have covered my eyes and peeped through my fingers to glimpse at my eternal home. But, I wasn't that brave. So I just laid there, waiting for something to happen.

The sounds were heavenly though. Crickets chirped, I heard waves. Then, I built up my courage and blinked. I saw stars twinkling like dancing diamonds in the sky. I blinked again, but this time, I shifted my eyes from left to right to get more of heaven's view. I saw the glow of the moon, and the glitter of the light bouncing off the water.

With the speed of a sloth, I opened my eyes wider.

Nurse ReAnn glided toward me, her feet barely touching the water beneath her. She looked radiant in her yellow celestial gown. The light of the moon emanated from her as she came toward me, smiling as her wings spread wide behind her. When she got close enough, she touched my hand. "Hi, Ms. Lachelle."

At first, I didn't say anything. *Can dead people talk?*

"Ms. Lachelle, you're not dead." She read my mind. "You are in a suspended state, between life and death. God knew that now was the time because you trusted me on earth. He knew you'd trust me here with our task."

"I'm not dead?" I asked.

"No, but this state cannot last long or you will die. I am your angel and I will facilitate our task. God has watched your faithfulness over the last few months. He wanted to reward you."

"Reward me? Why? I haven't been faithful, there were days when I wanted to give up. There were days when I was mad at Him."

"But you didn't give up, you prayed, you kept the faith; now God wants to reward you." Nurse ReAnn raised her arm and for the first time, I moved. I turned my head in the direction she pointed and saw a bright light leading to the moon. Then I saw his face, painted on the moon. My man, my love, my dead husband, Brian.

"My Chelle." I heard Brian's velvety tenor voice call me in that way that I thought I'd never hear again. God allowed me to hear his voice again; see his face again. If I was dreaming, I hoped I'd never wake up.

"I know you have been hurting, missing me. I've seen your tears and cries. But, through it all, you kept the faith, all for our baby."

"Brian." I was finally able to breathe his name. But I didn't want to do too much else. I didn't want to miss a moment with my love.

"Chelle, I need you to fight. I didn't have a chance to fight for my life. I want you to fight. Fight to kiss our baby girl. I want you to tell her how much her daddy will always love her." He paused. "I will love her to the moon and back."

He knew it was a girl. Until this moment only Dr. Price, Ms. Lori, Tracy, Vanessa, and John knew the gender of our baby.

"But Brian, you aren't here. I know I should be happy, but there are some days when..."

"You are lonely." He said what I couldn't bring myself to tell him. Brian continued, "God is faithful. He gives you what you need when you need it."

Was he talking about John?

"And remember, He began this good work in you and He will continue His work until it is finished." He paused as if he wanted that scripture to settle inside of me. "Will you fight for your life so that our daughter has one parent in the flesh?"

It was hard to fight. That took energy and Brian had been my energizer. His smile gave me life. "I'm torn between wanting to be with you and wanting to be there with our baby."

"That shouldn't be a conflict or a contest at all. You have to choose life -- your life and our baby's life."

I knew Brian's words were the truth, but I had to tell him my truth as well. "I want to be happy, darling, I really do. And there were days when I almost was, but I didn't want to betray you."

"Love is never a betrayal. I've felt your pain, I've seen your tears. But, for the sake of our daughter, you have to let go of the hurt and pain, knowing that a part of me is still there with you and will always be with you. I want you to be happy, and you just have to remember that God always has a plan."

As soon as Brian said those words, our eyes locked and together, we recited, "For I know the plans that I have for you, plans for good and not for disaster," like we had so many times before. There were tears in my eyes as he continued. "My Chelle, our baby girl has a future. You have a future, don't ever forget that. Please accept the future that God has promised."

His voice sounded farther away, but I could still hear him. "Have faith, keep the faith; faith alone will get you through this. Only. By. Faith."

I was getting ready to ask him how I could do that when his face began to fade. "No, Brian!" I called to him. I wasn't ready to let him go again.

"Ms. Lachelle." I heard Nurse ReAnn calling my name, but I didn't want to hear anything she had to say. I wanted to stay with Brian. "I must get you back. You cannot stay in this state any longer."

I blinked back tears as I thought about what my husband had said. If I fought, if I fought to stay alive for our baby and me, a piece of Brian would always be with me because of this time that God had graced me with. I couldn't waste these moments. I had to do what Brian said.

"Come on, Ms. Lachelle." Nurse ReAnn said, taking my hand.

I nodded, and inside I made a vow to Brian. *I will fight for my life and the life of our daughter, I promise you. I won't waste these gifts that God has given me. The gift of seeing you one more time and the gift of our daughter. I will do everything I can to show God that I appreciate this time that He gave us.*

As Nurse ReAnn pulled me away, my eyes stayed focused on the moon, even as Brian's face had completely faded away. And as my nurse took me back, I closed my eyes and now, talked to my daughter. "Baby Girl, we've got some work to do!"

Chapter 26

I was asleep, but I was awake. I could hear everything that was going on, but I couldn't say a thing. I could see, too, even though my eyes weren't open, they couldn't open.

It was scary, but then, it was not. I felt calm; I felt peace. I felt as if I should just lay there and listen to the doctors so they could do their work -- the work for me and my baby.

"Mrs. Jackson's vitals have stabilized."

That was Dr. Price's voice.

"Let's begin inducing the coma."

Oh, my God, a coma. I tried to frown, but nothing on me would move.

Dr. Price said, "If she remains in stable condition, throughout the day, we should be able to give Mrs. Jackson a very sweet Christmas gift."

The doctors went on to discuss when they would reconvene and then, I was left alone with just the machines that beeped with each of my heartbeats, and the nurses, who kept up a regular schedule checking on me. I waited to see Nurse ReAnn, but she wasn't among the staff. I hoped she would be there when it was time for my baby to be born.

Hours later, Dr. Price came back into the room, and I wanted to shout when I heard her tell the team, "She's strong enough. We can do this." Then, she leaned over me and said, "Hang in there, Mrs. Jackson; you're strong."

I wanted to tell her that I was strong, even stronger than she knew since I saw Brian. There were no doubts now -- I would do this.

I heard one of the nurses say the time. I felt the gentle movement of the bed. The wheels squeaked as they rolled me down the bright hallway. I started to feel anxious, but then I reminded myself to stay calm. Breathe. Just breathe. Finally, we arrived in the operating room. Although they placed my bed under a light, it was cold.

"Mrs. Jackson, I hope you can hear me. We will begin your caesarian section now."

I didn't feel anything, but I smelled something burning. Half of the staff was focused on Dr. Price's hands while the other half was focused on the machines' monitors, blinking and beeping. No one seemed concerned about the smell. Again, I told myself to breathe, just breathe.

Suddenly, everyone in the room heard the loud cries of the baby. My baby. The doctors and the nurses shouted a collective, "Yes." Dr. Price delivered my little Christmas package to a nurse. As she cleaned her up, a tear streamed down her cheek, as I heard her say, "The miracle of Christmas."

"Let's get her to the NICU for examination," said Dr. Price. I was glad that Dr. Price had already explained to me what would happen in the operating room because her instruction, to the nurse, would've alarmed me if I didn't know that all premature babies were taken to the neonatal intensive care unit immediately after birth.

For the first time in a long time, I was happy. This was why Brian wanted me to fight. He wanted me to live to see the plan that God had for me. As sleep eased into my body, I clung to one of Brian's last phrases. "Faith alone..."

Chapter 27

"Mrs. Jackson, Mrs. Jackson." I heard a voice shouting. My eyes widened enough for me to see a nurse opening the blinds. I squinted as the light filtered through.

"Merry Christmas, Mrs. Jackson." My eyes shot open.

Then, I remembered, and I lifted my hand to my belly. "Faith." I whispered in a raspy voice.

"Shhhh." The nurse directed. "Your baby girl is here, weighing in at five pounds and three ounces and very healthy. Her lungs are strong, trust me. She gave us a very determined cry."

I smiled, but then suddenly, I was overcome with exhaustion. Right before I closed my eyes, I wondered, *Where is Nurse ReAnn?*

In my sleep, more dreams came to me -- Nurse ReAnn and Brian. Had I seen my husband? Had I dreamed about him? My questions were many, but my sleep was filled with peace.

When I awakened, the sun's rays brightened my room, and my eyes fell to the white bassinet beside my bed.

"Oh." I whispered.

"Let me help you sit up." A nurse whom I didn't recognize was in my room monitoring the machines.

The only thing I wanted to do was cradle my baby girl. This was a dream come true. "Can I hold her?"

"I'll give her to you."

Sliding her right hand under her head and the other under her bottom, she placed her in my arms.

I looked at my baby. I had a baby. Life had new meaning. I had someone to love again.

"Hi, baby." I cradled her. Her little eyes struggled to open, and she gazed at me as though she knew me. I stroked her smooth skin. "I wish that I had been the first person to hold you. But now, I'll never let you go." I took in the soft, pale pink preemie onesie that she was wearing. "Where did you get this cute little 'Baby's First Christmas' bonnet?" As I stroked the bonnet, I noticed the yellow wings on the side. That made me blink, and I remembered -- Nurse ReAnn...in my dream...and her wings.

"It wasn't a dream." I whispered. "Nurse ReAnn was my angel."

As I secured her in my arms, I remembered Brian's last words to me. *Have faith. Keep the faith. Faith alone.*

"Baby girl, your daddy gave me your name. My baby, Faith." I nuzzled my cheek against her cheek.

"I'm going to leave you and the baby alone now. Is there anything you'd like me to get for you?" She asked over her red bifocals.

I shook my head. I didn't need anything else. God gave me the best Christmas gift.

She left and not even five minutes later I noticed the door sliding open. John popped his head through the door. "Can I come in for a minute?"

I smiled, remembering what Brian said. *"God is faithful. He gives you what you need when you need it."*

I shook my head.

His crumpled clothes told the story of his six feet and seven-inch frame crammed into a chair waiting for good news. He threw his jacket in the empty chair in my room.

Before he sat down in it, he stole a look at my baby girl.

"She's precious." he whispered.

"How long have you been here?" I asked.

"Most of the night. Tracy and Vanessa are in the waiting area still asleep. I had to tip in here. You know Tracy wasn't having me seeing you first this time."

"Y'all are getting along so well."

His laugh was his agreement. "I can't stay. I'm gonna get out of here and run through my mom's house. My daughter will probably be waking up soon, and I want to be there when she does. She knows I'm Santa, but you know how ten-year-old girls can be. 'Where's Daddy?'" He mocked her, taking his voice up at least five octaves. "I've been in different cities most of her life. Now I finally get the time to be home for the holidays and that's important to me."

"I hope I get to meet her one day."

"Oh, you will. The family calls her the baby whisperer. I believe you two will get along well."

His sincerity, his love showed in his eyes.

"Do you have a name for her yet?"

"I'm mulling over one in particular."

He got up to wash his hands at the sink in the small bathroom off the room and then, he stood at the side of my bed.

"Can I hold her before I leave?"

"You may." I said extending my arms to him.

John sat down and focused on her.

"Hey beautiful, just like your momma."

The baby looked up at John as he spoke. "You are a precious gift from God. Your mother kept the faith. Faith alone was what she leaned on."

Faith alone. Brian used the same phrase.

"I'm gonna give you back to your momma now. But, I'll see you soon, okay?"

After he placed her back in my arms, he grabbed his jacket.

Before he slipped out of the door, I said, "Faith, say goodbye to John."

His face lit up as bright as a Christmas tree. Then he ducked out of the hospital room door.

Turning my attention to the joy in my arms, I spoke to my daughter. "Baby, I hope you like the name Faith because, without faith, nothing is possible. We've been through a lot and with God, we'll get through anything. And we have a heavenly angel, your dad." Then, I paused. "No, we have two heavenly angels, your daddy, and our nurse. They will always watch over us."

As I rocked Faith in my arms, I heard Eddie Kendrick's smooth tenor, falsetto voice singing *Silent Night,* coming from the nurses' station.

I sang along: "*Round yon Virgin Mother and Child. Holy Infant so tender and mild...*"

For the first time, I smiled, I really smiled. "Faith, we had anything but a silent night."

Epilogue

Easter Sunday at Divine Restoration Christian Ministries was alive with shouts of "Thank-you Jesus" and "He is risen" as Pastor Smith rose to the pulpit. Vibrant colored dresses, hats and suits filled the sanctuary as people walked the aisles praising and worshiping God. The praise was so high that Pastor Smith signaled Brother Jones, the Minister of Music, to strike up the sound.

After throwing his arms up into the air, the choir jumped up and the sweet sound of Kirk Franklin's 'Don't Cry' brought most of the congregation to their feet. Vanessa and I stood amidst the praise and worship with outstretched arms. Tracy held Faith, rocking to the music.

"Give Him praise. Give. Him. The. Praise." Pastor encouraged everyone to get their shout on, and they did, up and down the aisles. The emotional frenzy continued until he instructed the band to bring the sound down.

As the choir sang the last melody, Pastor Smith spoke. "Why do you cry? He has risen. Why are you weeping? He's. Not. Dead!"

The spirit was still high with praise and worship as shouts of "For me." and "Thank-you, Jesus." echoed throughout the congregation.

Pastor Smith stood behind the large wooden pulpit as the thankful cries dissipated. "I have a Word from the Lord. But before I begin preaching I'd like to bring up a family today for an Easter Sunday baby dedication."

My village showed up for Faith's dedication; even Keisha sauntered down the aisle with a skirt that met her knee and a jacket to cover her chest. As I looked at the faces of my co-workers, extended family from out of town, and my church family, there was one face missing.

John had traveled to Dallas to deliver Easter Baskets on behalf of his foundation. He scheduled an early flight back this morning so that he'd make Faith's dedication. I reached in my bag and pulled my phone from my purse, no message.

"Can the Jackson family come up and join me?" As Pastor walked down the steps from the pulpit he continued speaking into his lapel microphone. "Today we'll dedicate Little Miss Faith Jackson. It *would* be a bittersweet day but since we're celebrating what Christ did for us on the cross, we know that Faith's earthly father is in heaven rejoicing on this day, too."

Before we stood, I smoothed the multiple ruffles on Faith's dress. A lilac sash adorned it at the waist with a matching flower on the side. Tracy untied the bonnet to make it easier for Pastor when it was time to anoint her head with oil. "She doesn't like this thing anyway," Tracy said hoping to give Faith some relief.

Over the past four months, I pondered who would be the godparents. I couldn't choose between Tracy and Vanessa. They would both be aunties to Faith anyway. Lady Kendra and I developed an unbreakable bond. When I thought about Pastor Smith, I knew that he would guide Faith's Christian walk and that Brian would approve of them. I asked them to be Faith's godparents and they humbly accepted.

"Everybody come on up, don't be shy."

After we assembled below the pulpit, Tracy handed Faith to First Lady Kendra who immediately broke out in baby talk, cooing to Faith who shared a big smile in return.

As Pastor began to speak, the chill of the early April morning wind blew through the church since the doors between the sanctuary and the foyer were propped open. Everyone looked back as John entered trying to be as inconspicuous as possible. But how could he be at six feet seven inches?

Tracy waved him down to the front and he stood with my village next to Aunt Louise who had kept her promise to be there for us. She traveled from Philly to D.C. twice a month to help me with the baby.

During one of our late night talks, I shared with her the 'John story'. She told me, "Chile, there is no shame or guilt in that. Do what God leads you to do. My nephew loved you, but he is gone now."

So she felt comfortable prodding him to move closer to us. "Go on over there boy. Take your place."

Before moving, he looked at me with a 'Can I?' expression etched on his face. With a look of approval, I waved him over and he stood right next to Tracy and Vanessa.

Pastor Smith shook John's hand which meant a lot to me. It was as if Pastor gave John his approval to become a part of my village. Lady Kendra sensed my emotions and rubbed my back to get me through.

"Now that we are all here we can dedicate little Miss Faith." Everyone seemed to straighten up in their seats.

"As you know in the Baptist tradition we don't baptize babies. We allow them to grow older to make their public profession of faith."

Pastor turned to pick up a small bowl from the altar. "Lachelle, what name have you given your baby girl?"

"I have named her Faith Briana Jackson."

"And what do those names mean?"

Faith alone.

"Faith means a strong belief in God and Briana means strong."

"It is important that we understand what we are calling our children. They need to know and understand the strength and power that lies in their names." He paused through a flurry of, "Amens." He continued. "Our Father in heaven, ordained baptism to signify our union with Christ and our cleansing from sin. Today we dedicate Faith and anoint and pray over her with a commitment from parents, godparents, and the village to share our faith and guide her life using Christian precepts and principles. We ask the Holy Spirit to guide and protect her throughout her development and allow her to become a Proverb thirty-one woman."

This was really happening. God is faithful.

"An old African proverb says that it takes a village to raise a child. Faith has a village here at her church, with her blood family and aunties and uncles who will care for her." As Pastor Smith anointed us with oil, he continued. "We ask that you bless Faith today so that she is safe from all harm and danger."

Looking over my entire village he asked, "Can I get an Amen?"

We all gave a resounding "Amen."

"Everyone may be seated and I'll deliver this Easter morning message from on high."

As we walked to our seats I couldn't help but notice the stream of light filtering through the multi-colored stained glass window right above our seats. It warmed my face once I sat.

I looked over my village and knew that Faith and I had made it through the storm. As her head rested on my shoulder I stroked her back and knew that God's grace and mercy would continue to bring us through, with faith alone.

I hope you enjoyed Lachelle's story.
Please tell a friend and leave a reveiw.
Coming soon,

The Switch.

<u>Read an excerpt</u>
July 1, 2017

"Today was a good day."

Ice Cube's vibrato bounced through the speakers of my SUV as I watched Lachelle enter the lobby of her ten story condominium. Once she stepped inside and waved *bye*, I gave her the peace sign and hit the gas pedal. The windshield wipers automatically cleaned the early morning dew from the glass. Even though Ice Cube's declaration was in past tense, I felt that I'd have a good day and it was only nine-thirty in the morning.

Today marked what would have been the twenty-fourth birthday of our son, Christian. Gravesite visits were my way of atoning for not being present on the day of his birth which was also the day of his death. That's the least a father could do.

But this year was different. Christian's mother, Lachelle, and I visited him together. We were high school sweethearts who lost touch after our baby was born. I shouldn't even say lost touch. That's a cop out. I'll re-phrase. I had just left for college.

And after my mother told me that Lachelle lost our baby I wasn't mature enough to come home and check on her. But I never stopped thinking about her.

Days turned to months and months turned into years. I graduated from college and was drafted into the NBA. Lachelle completed her degree a year after I did and got married a few years later. Lachelle's husband was murdered last year. I've been nothing but a gentleman as she grieved.

After twenty-four years, Lachelle and I had our own baggage but were lightening our loads. I was feeling her and she was feeling me.

People thought luck brought Lachelle and I together at Christian's gravesite a year ago today. But I knew it was divine intervention.

The ring from my cell phone through the car speakers diverted my attention to my dash board. It was Smitty, my agent, probably calling to press me about the ESPN interview on Monday morning. This brotha could be worse than a nagging woman sometimes.

I pressed the green phone button on my dash. "What's up, Smitty?" I'd known William Smith, hence Smitty, since my sophomore year at University of Kentucky. I was the athlete and he was the scholar. In the hood you got girls one of two ways: athletics or money. Smitty kept it real. He knew he'd never get girls by balling. And he was an average looking dude with an average sense of humor. So he set his sights on earning his law degree to get the attention of the ladies. And he succeeded.

"My man, fifty grand." Smitty's southern drawl echoed through my truck as I dashed through the yellow light five minutes from home. "Did you handle your business this morning?"

I knew he wouldn't go straight into the business of the day. But, it was coming soon.

"I made my annual pilgrimage. But Lachelle and I went together. It was a good visit."

"Yo dog, you smash yet?"

His filter was nonexistent. "Dog, I'm really into her, don't ask me that. And besides we're Christians."

He was quiet for a moment. I knew that meant trouble. He finally responded. "Don't Christians smash?"

I thought about pushing the red phone button on the dash board to end this conversation. But instead, I waved at the guard as I entered my gated community and continued talking. "Dude, what was the purpose of your call? I'm walking into the house now. I'd like to shower and grab some grub before I leave for New York."

I hadn't gotten to the front door yet, but I needed to hurry him off the phone before I lost it.

"So you're ready? Packed and everything? We're meeting a few of the ESPN head honchos tonight for dinner. It'll be a non-interview, interview."

This was the epitome of our friendship, Smitty feeling like he had to water everything down for me.

"Yes, Smitty. You've told me that, a few times. And before you ask, I have the itinerary and the tickets your assistant sent."

"Okay, dude. I'll let you go get to it." He responded.

After removing the audio from the blue tooth, I pulled the phone to my ear and jumped out of the truck. "I'll get up wit' you later."

He ended the call with our customary sign-off. "Holla back."

As I jogged up the sidewalk, the sprinklers ignited. Note to self: contact the landscapers to lower the sensitivity.

"Hel-lo." I had this habit of coming into my empty house, announcing my entrance. The echo bounced. Boxes lined the walls. If I was gonna live between DC and NYC, I might rent this house out and lease a downtown condo . Of course it would need to have a state of the art gym. But first things first, I had to land this gig. ESPN approached me to work as a sports analyst/commentator. Talking about the game of basketball...heaven.

I grabbed an apple out of the fridge and ran up the stairs to the master bedroom. The view overlooked the Potomac River. God blessed me with a skill and a career that allowed me to travel the world. Determining where to retire wasn't a hard decision. My daughter, Hope, lived here with my ex-wife and bonding with her was the major reason I knew I'd settle here. The other reasons were Lachelle and her baby girl, Faith. But again, first things first.

My Acela train rolled out of Union Station at 1:30pm. I still had time to get there. Before showering I turned on the TV and the local news blared.

After showering, I went into my walk-in closet. Comfortable khakis and a polo shirt would do. While sitting on the edge of my bed, I heard the music that accompanied the breaking news segments. It drew my attention to the TV.

The reporter delved right into the story. "We have breaking news regarding baby switching allegations at the Sibley Memorial Hospital here in Washington, D.C. This, allegedly, took place in 1993 during the months of May through July. It has not been reported how many babies were switched but as one family stated, 'even one baby is too many.' There are reports of bribery from families to switch infants due to known illnesses of their babies or even stillborn babies."

My shirt that I was about to throw over my head dropped to the floor.

Summer 1993. Sibley Hospital. Baby switching.

Dumbfounded, I sat on the edge of the bed for a minute. Christian was born at Sibley Hospital during the summer of 1993 but I needed to confirm that with Lachelle because maybe I was trippn'. I picked up the phone to call her but it slipped from my trembling hand.

Before I picked up the phone I snatched the remote off the pillow next to me. I replayed the breaking news segment.

Summer 1993. Sibley Hospital. Baby switching.

I couldn't call her, she'd detect the anxiety in my voice. I picked up the phone and sent a simple text to ask a simple question. *Where was Christian born?* The answer might prove to alter the trajectory of our lives.

The *delivered* prompt popped up on the phone.

I picked my shirt up and continued getting dressed.

Lachelle typically answered right back.

As I rubbed oil on my hands to run through my hair, I heard the text alert.

I oiled my hair and viewed her response.

Did we just visit our son or someone else's?

Made in the USA
Middletown, DE
19 April 2023

29085343R00106